Coffee To Go,
With a Spaceship

Book Two

in the
Galactic Smugglers for Hire
series

M.J. Wahl

FRANKLIN STREET PRESS

Cover Design by eBooklaunch
www.ebooklaunch.com

Copyright © 2017, 2024 by MJ Wahl
Paperback ISBN 978-0-993708992
6x9 print version

Published by Franklin Street Press
*** ***

www.mjwahl.com

Also by M.J. Wahl

Aliens, Spaceships and the Occasional Latte
Octavia Seven
Heretic
The Tolerance Bureau

For Eli & Jen

Coffee To Go,
With a Spaceship

CHAPTER ONE

THE LITTLE MAN sitting across from me looked suspiciously like an elf. Now, to the best of my knowledge I had never met an elf before, so I suppose I didn't really know what one might look like. But still, it seemed to me that all he lacked was a green coat with brass buttons to pass as one of Santa's helpers.

His short legs hung freely from the chair he sat in, and he swung them back and forth as he chattered away. A leather cap adorned the top of his long narrow face. The cap had flaps that conveniently covered the tops of his ears, but I was ready to bet a week's pay that they were pointed.

He wore a brown leather tunic with a belt and straps holding little pouches. A pair of round goggles were pushed up onto the cap. His leggings were of some black material that looked like leather. I half expected to find little green pointed boots on his feet, but instead he wore very sturdy looking hikers.

Now I didn't believe in elves and had no reason to expect one to visit my office, but then up until six months ago I didn't believe in space aliens either. But all that changed when I met the Radauti last summer. Since then I've become a much more open-minded individual.

"Excuse me," he said, interrupting my thoughts. "I'm not sure I've entirely got your attention." He coughed and his eyes glowered at me from under eyebrows that stuck out almost as far as his beaked nose.

"Um, sorry. I guess I was a bit distracted," I said.

The little fellow had walked into the office unannounced not twenty minutes ago, catching me in the front reception area where Donna normally sat. Unfortunately, Donna wasn't in, so I was left to make coffee and fend for myself. So I was alone in the reception room making coffee when this little guy in leather breeches walked in. He introduced himself as Montclair, bowed deeply, and stated that he would like to hire me. I was much too stunned by the appearance of a midget in medieval garb to think of a polite way to get rid of him, so we went into my office and sat down to talk.

And that is how I found myself with the strange little guy across from me.

"As I was saying, it's imperative that I engage your services forthwith. And I'm prepared to pay handsomely for them."

Forthwith? Who uses words like that anymore? I thought. Then I asked: "What exactly are the services you require?"

"I've explained that already. I need you to recover an object that's been stolen from us."

"I know, but you've been hazy on the details. What sort of object?"

He reached into his tunic and brought out a folded sheet of paper. He hopped down from his chair and stepped up to my desk. His head wasn't much higher than the desk. He slapped the paper down and returned to his seat. I reached across the desk, picked it up and unfolded it.

It was a photograph of a large piece of jewelry. I looked at the picture as he described it. "It's a fifty-five-carat diamond set in a gold brooch. The chain is sterling silver."

He continued talking but I quickly held up a hand. "Did you say fifty-five carats?"

"Ah, yes."

"That makes it bigger than the Hope Diamond, the biggest diamond in the world."

"If you say so. I've never heard of the Hope Diamond."

I just stared at him. He started talking again, but I wasn't listening, too much in shock at the outrageous claim.

I interrupted him again. "And this diamond, which you claim is bigger than the Hope, which no one has ever heard of before. You want me to find it?"

"Absolutely! It must be recovered. It's been in the family for thirty-six generations. Of course, its value goes far beyond mere monetary worth. It also has magical properties."

I stared into his pointy little face. "Magical, huh?"

He nodded solemnly.

I massaged my right temple. "So let me get this straight. You claim to have had in your family for over thirty generation..."

"Thirty-six," he corrected me.

"Thirty-six. Right. So easily for a thousand years or more, you've had in your family a diamond you claim is bigger than the Hope Diamond."

"Precisely."

"And so why haven't I or anyone else ever heard of this diamond? It should be world famous, like the Hope."

"I can't help what people have or haven't heard of before," he said.

"And you also claim it has magical properties?"

"Yes! That's why it's imperative that we recover it as quickly as possible."

This guy is a fruitcake, I thought. *Time to get rid of him*. I stood up, hoping he'd get the hint and leave without any more fuss. "I'm very sorry, but I already have a very heavy caseload and couldn't possibly take on any more work. Maybe you should go to the police with this."

It was a lie, of course. I didn't have a heavy caseload. In fact, I didn't have any cases and had nothing better to do but sit in the office drinking coffee and doing crosswords.

He remained seated and his bright eyes fixed on me. Then he brought a little fist up to his mouth and coughed. "I'd prefer you take the case. Gluplock recommended you very highly, and I don't think the police would appreciate some of the finer nuances of my situation."

That got my attention. "Gluplock? How do you know about him?" I asked slowly. Only four other people on Earth knew about my alien friends.

He nodded. "You came very highly recommended."

I sat back down. "You know Gluplock?" I asked slowly.

"Well, not exactly. He's more of a friend of a friend."

"I see. And this friend of yours, who is a friend of Gluplock...who exactly is he?"

"Another Radauti trader, like Gluplock."

I looked Montclair over and his other-worldly strangeness started to make sense. "Where exactly did you say you're from?"

"A nice little world thirty odd light-years from here." He pulled his coat a little tighter across his middle. "And I must say, our winters are much more temperate than yours."

I suppose I should have known better since getting to know my alien friends, but I couldn't help feeling surprised. I still didn't expect people from other planets to walk into my office.

After a moment I said: "So this missing brooch is on your world?"

"I certainly hope so."

"And you came all the way here to Earth to find me, and talk me into going back to your planet to look for it?"

"Yes. Precisely," he said brightly, as if it were an entirely normal thing.

"Don't they have something like police or detectives on your world?"

"Well, yes, of a sort. But as I said, the circumstances require your specialized expertise, and you came very highly recommended."

"That must have been a pretty good recommendation for you to come all the way to Earth," I said.

He nodded. "Indeed."

It didn't take me long to make a decision. As soon as he mentioned space, I knew I wasn't interested. I had been holding the photograph in my hand through the entire bizarre conversation. Now I released it and let it drop to the desk. "Sorry, I can't help you."

His eyes looked like they might pop out of his head. "The fee I am prepared to offer is a small fortune on your world."

I shook my head. "I won't go back into space for any price. There are things out there that want to kill me. And the last time I went into space, some of them followed me back here. I don't need the complications. Sorry."

"Oh come now. You won't be gone more than a few weeks."

"I don't need the money, and I have a son to think about and I don't want to be away that long." And Donna, I added silently, but Montclair didn't need to know about us. I didn't want to be away from her either. The last time I disappeared into space, it had put her through a horrible ordeal and I couldn't do that to her again. And I had attracted the attention of some very nasty alien bounty hunters. Who needs that kind of trouble?

And the truth was I didn't need the money. Donna and I had a nice little business on the side selling coffee to nice, peace-loving aliens. The kind that didn't want to put us on their dinner menu and were happy to pay us a handsome fee for our coffee.

Apparently, you can't get coffee on any other planet but Earth, which worked out just fine for me and Donna. We split the profits evenly and were making more money than we ever dreamed possible. We were even planning on retiring from the PI business. Donna wanted to spend more time looking after the farm where she lived with her mother.

I still hadn't decided what I was going to do, but with a girlfriend and a son firmly entrenched in town, I wasn't going far. Not yet, anyway. Not until Johnnie was old enough to decide for himself if he wanted to come with us.

I could tell by his look that he wasn't about to take 'no' for an answer. Just as I was trying to figure out a way to get rid of him, my Samsung started vibrating on the desk in front of me. Normally I would ignore it when I was with a client, but this was a perfect opportunity to bring the interview to an end. The timing couldn't have been better.

The display said caller unknown. I answered it anyway, silently thankful.

"Jack Winters," I said into the phone, looking at Montclair who glared back at me.

"Mister Winters?"

"Yes."

"This is Carrie. You need to get over here right away. Something's happened," the voice on the other end shouted in panic.

I frowned. "Who's this?"

"Carrie, remember. I live next door to Gilda and I babysit Johnnie."

"Oh, right. Sure, I remember. What is..."

But she cut me off. "I'm at Gilda's now. You need to get over here right away. Her place is, like, trashed. And I can't find Johnnie anywhere."

My back went stiff. "Okay, slow down. What do you mean?"

"I mean, like, Johnnie isn't here."

"Is he outside playing, or maybe over at a friend's?"

"No Mister Winters. I don't think you understand. The house is totally trashed. Furniture smashed and everything. And Gilda is here next to me crying and saying they took him."

I jumped up from my chair. "Who took Johnnie?"

"I don't know, and what Gilda says makes no sense. Something about giant monkeys."

I didn't even bother to try and process that. Instead, I said: "Have you looked through the house?"

"Yeah, and he's nowhere. I'm really worried that something bad has happened to him."

"Have you called the police?"

"Yeah, as soon as I got here and saw what happened."

"Good. I'll be right down. Stay with Gilda until I get there, okay?"

"Okay, for sure."

I stuck the phone in a pocket. Then I said to Montclair as I strapped my shoulder harness on: "I'm sorry to cut our visit short, but I need to run."

I pulled my Ruger Blackhawk 44 out of a drawer and checked the cylinder to be sure, but I already knew it was loaded. Montclair sputtered with indignation. "But I travelled all the way to Earth to engage your services!"

I slipped it into the shoulder harness. "I'm sorry you wasted your time, but I'm not going back into space. Ever. Too many nasty ways to die."

He stood up and straightened his tunic. "That is your final answer then?"

"Yes," I said as I slipped on my jacket and headed for the door. "I have to hurry. You can see yourself out." I left him standing in my office and ran for the front door.

∞

The police hadn't arrived yet when I pulled up in front of Gilda's bungalow, but neighbors had started to gather on the sidewalk in front of her porch. She lived in a nice little neighborhood of older homes built in the 20's and 30's. Lots of big trees and front porches and families with young kids and older retired couples. Crime was low so when something did happen it generated a lot of excitement.

Parked cars lined both sides of the street, so I double parked and got out. I had to push my way through the crowd. Some of them recognized me and wanted to talk, but I kept going.

The front door was gone, completely blown off its hinges. The brick surrounding where the doorframe used to be was scorched black and looked like it had been mauled by a jack hammer.

I went through the threshold, stepping on pieces of wood and glass. The walls in the hallway around me had deep gouges, like they'd been slashed by a very strong man with a big crowbar.

Or a very large animal with massive claws.

I could see down the hall into the kitchen. The fridge lay on its side across the floor with the door open. The contents had fallen out and milk ran over the floor. The kitchen table was overturned and chairs scattered. Carrie hadn't exaggerated when she said the place was trashed.

"Gilda!" I called. "It's me, Jack."

Carrie answered from the living room down the hall. "We're in here."

I went into the living room and found Gilda curled up in a tight ball on the floor, in front of the couch. The couch had been slashed and turned over. Cushion material squeezed out from dozens of rips. Carrie sat on the floor next to Gilda with a comforting hand on her shoulder.

The living room didn't look any better than the kitchen or hallway. The loveseat Gilda and I had bought in happier times was crushed. Someone or something had actually snapped its frame and crushed it. The coffee table was in pieces, its glass top shattered and metal frame broken. Papers, magazines, broken picture frames, and glass littered the floor.

I went over to Gilda and knelt before her and looked into her face. She looked unharmed, but her eyes were swollen and red from tears and she trembled. She stared blankly into space behind me.

I touched her arm. "Gilda, what happened?"

Her eyes slowly moved from the empty space she had been staring at to me. She started to sputter, as if trying to force words that wouldn't come, or trying to utter the unimaginable.

"Th..th..thi..things c-c-c-came and...and..." Spittle dribbled from the side of her mouth. I gave her shoulder a squeeze. "It's okay, they're gone."

"And...th-they t-t-took him."

"Took Johnnie?"

She nodded and fresh tears poured down her face. "Oh my God Jack they were horrible."

"Who?"

"I-I-I d-d-don't k-k-know. Things. H-h-hideous t-t-things."

Carrie patted Gilda's shoulder and looked at me. "She's been going on about giant monkeys since I got here. It doesn't make any sense."

Gilda raised a hand and pointed at something behind me. "T-they w-w-wrote th-th-that," she said.

I turned around to look. She used to keep pictures on that wall, but they'd all been knocked down, replaced by strange black markings. At first they looked random. Short lines at different angles, interspersed with dashes and other symbols, as if a drunk had tried to scribble. But as I stared at it I noticed organised patterns. It was some sort of writing, but not in any alphabet I'd ever seen.

I looked around the place and a chill went down my back. I got a bad feeling. *Giant monkeys.* I thought of them as a cross between a giant toad and a gorilla, but that's just me.

There was one way to find out, but I didn't want Carrie to see what I had to show Gilda. Looking at Carrie I said: "Do you mind going into the kitchen and finding something to calm Gilda's nerves. I think you'll find a bottle of brandy in the cupboard over the sink."

"Oh sure," she said and got up from the floor.

When she was gone, I pulled out my phone and opened the picture gallery. I still kept some photos, for some morbid reason, of the things I'd encountered in space. The same things that had followed me back to Earth and tried to kill Donna and myself on her mother's farm last summer.

I opened up a picture and turned the phone to her. "Is this what they looked like?"

It was a close-up of an alien bounty-hunter I'd shot on Beatrice's farm last summer, after a group of them had come to Earth gunning for me. Its face was something like a cross between a giant toad and an ape.

She stared at the phone for a moment, then her eyes went wide with recognition and horror. She nodded furiously. "Yes! Yes! That's them!"

I put the phone back in my pocket and slumped against an overturned chair. I suddenly felt very weak and started to shake. The Rajnack had Johnnie.

But she sat bolt upright and looked at me with cold, hard eyes. "Y-y-you have pictures? H-h-ow could you possibly have pictures of those monsters?"

My mouth went dry and my voice cracked. "That's a bit hard to explain, but I know who took our son."

She pointed accusingly. "You! I knew this had something to do with you! I don't know how, but somehow this is your fault."

She was right. In a sense, this was my fault. The Rajnack had originally come to Earth because of me, and now more must have followed. I was the connection.

But I could hardly tell Gilda any of that. "Don't be ridiculous," I said weakly.

"How else could you happen to have pictures of them? You must know more than you're telling me," she shouted, suddenly very coherent. Anger tends to focus the mind.

Carrie arrived with a drink and handed it to Gilda. She took it and set it with a bang on the floor, never taking her eyes off of me. "I'm calling the police," she spat at me and got up from the floor.

"I've already called them," Carrie said.

"Well, what's taking them so long? Where's my phone," she said to no one in particular and stormed out of the living room.

I looked up at Carrie from my sitting position on the floor. She looked back at me with sympathetic eyes. "You look like you need a drink too."

I decided I wasn't going to accomplish anything by curling up on the floor and sucking my thumb, as much as I felt like doing exactly like. I needed to start looking for Johnnie right away.

I stood up and looked around the room, surveying the wreckage, and then looked at Carrie. I'd known her for several years. She was about seventeen and lived next door with her parents and often babysat Johnnie.

"What can you tell me? Did you see or hear anything? Any detail will help."

She nodded. "Oh yeah. Like, it sounded like someone was going crazy in here. I could hear the banging and crashing from next door."

"Did you see anyone else?"

She shook her head. "No, they were gone by the time I got here."

"Did you come in through the front?"

"Yeah."

"How long was it between the time you heard the noise and when you came over?"

"Not long. Like, maybe a few minutes."

I looked towards the back of the house where a door led outside to a small yard. From there, a gate led into an alley that ran behind the houses on the block. "They must have left by the back door, otherwise you would have seen them on your way in." I left Carrie and followed the trail of debris through the house towards the back.

Something crunched under my foot and I looked down. It was a picture of Johnnie in a smashed frame covered in broken glass. I bent over, brushed away the shards of glass and picked up the photo. He was standing in his Little Jays uniform holding a bat and wearing a red baseball cap. I remembered that game and started to ache all over. After a moment I set the picture down.

The back door was open and surprisingly still on its hinges. I stepped onto the small porch and looked over the yard. It wasn't very big, and everything seemed to be in its place. I walked out into the yard and looked around for some kind of sign, any clue that might help. Finally I stopped in the middle of the yard and looked straight up into the sky, for no better reason than I was pretty sure that's where they'd taken my son.

I thought about that while looking up into the clouds. It made no sense. The Rajnack wanted me dead, so why had they come to take Johnnie? Was Johnnie even still alive? I had no idea, but for the moment I'd operate on the assumption they hadn't killed him. And if they hadn't killed him, they wanted him alive for some reason. That reason was most likely me. Maybe they were still pissed with me for killing off their spawn-sister on the planet Carimeth.

So why didn't they just come after me? There were a lot of things I didn't have answers to yet. Hopefully they would get a hold of me soon and let me know their demands.

I was still looking up at the sky when a voice interrupted my thoughts. "You don't expect to find Johnnie in the clouds, do you?"

I looked. A cop in a dark blue trench coat stood on the back porch staring down at me.

∞

"Detective Wolfowitz," I said. "It's about time you guys showed up. What took so long?"

Wolfowitz ignored the question and walked down the steps to join me in the backyard. He pulled a stick of gum out from a pocket and slowly, methodically unwrapped it. "I had a chat with your ex while you were out here daydreaming in the clouds," he said and folded the gum into his mouth.

I waited for his point. There was always a point with Wolfowitz. "And?" I said.

"And she thinks you know something about this."

"Gilda's welcome to think whatever she wants," I retorted. "She likes to blame me for everything."

He raised an eyebrow. "Who said anything about blame?"

"Believe me, that's exactly what she meant. Did she also tell you that it was a pair of giant monkeys that stole Johnnie?"

"She mentioned something about that, yeah."

I chuckled, trying to laugh it off, but I'm a bad actor and not so sure how convincing I was. "There, you see? Giant monkeys."

He chewed thoughtfully. "Yeah, it sounds crazy and normally I would put it down to frayed nerves. She's just been through a lot. But here's the thing. Her description just happens to line up with a few other things I've heard."

"Like what?" I asked, feeling like a deer caught in the headlights of an on-rushing train. I knew all about the aliens that looked like ugly apes, but was still trying to play dumb. I mean, it's not exactly the kind of thing you can share on Facebook or tell the police and expect to be taken seriously.

He chewed gum thoughtfully for a moment before he said: "This naked man walks into the police station of a small town in Saskatchewan."

"This sounds like the beginning of a bad joke," I said.

He raised a hand. "Just listen. This town is real small. I've never even heard of it before. This naked guy comes up to the desk sergeant, blubbering about spaceships and aliens and giant toad things with laser guns. I mean, he's completely hysterical, shaking all over."

"So?"

"So, he claims to be from Hamilton. So the cops call here and unfortunately I happen to be in the office at the wrong time and the call gets routed to me. And I end up having to talk to the guy for a bit, in order to ascertain who he is and what we should do with him."

The naked guy in Saskatchewan had to be Alex Crowley, I realized with a shock. After the incident on the farm, my alien friends said they would strip Alex naked and leave him in Saskatchewan as punishment. He did try to kill me, after all. I started to get a bad feeling, but gamely continued to play dumb. I wasn't going down without a fight.

"I don't understand what this has to do with me," I said. "Why do you care about the ravings of a naked guy in Saskatchewan who claims to have seen flying saucers?"

"He claims to know you. Called you by name. Said there was a gunfight on your girlfriend's farm with big toads."

"Sounds nuts," I said.

"Yeah, that's what I thought too. Except how does he know you? And how could he know about the incident on your farm?"

"There was no incident on Donna's farm."

"That's not what her neighbors say. I did some digging and found recordings of numerous 911 calls that afternoon from people who swear they heard shooting and explosions."

"We were having a party. What they heard was fireworks."

Then he dropped the bomb. "That's not what Beatrice said. She called 911 too, and swore giant toads were attacking her farm."

Damn. I'd forgotten about Beatrice, Donna's mother. She'd called 911 too that afternoon, although at the time the 911 operator just laughed and hung up on her.

"And another 911 call from a guy driving by in a van, scared out of his wits, describing ape-like things running around the yard."

"It still sounds nuts. Come on Wolfowitz. You're not really taking any of this seriously?"

"I take seriously the fact that your son is missing and Missus Winters place has been ransacked."

I stared at him. "Not as seriously as I take it. But I don't know anything about giant monkeys."

"Well, here's the thing. The description from the 911 calls lined up exactly with the naked guy's story in Saskatchewan. How could he possibly know about that unless he was really there and saw what he saw? And now your ex-wife's description is very similar. Strange, eh?"

"What do you want me to say, Detective? Can we just get on with finding Johnnie?"

He held up a hand. "If it was just one person, I'd agree. But three different people, completely unrelated with no chance of collusion, all say the same thing. And give very similar descriptions of these creatures."

"You don't really believe in these giant toad stories, do you?" I laughed, trying to fake it. But like I said, I'm a bad actor.

"I don't know what I believe. Maybe they were guys in gorilla costumes. Last year there were a string of bank robberies by guys dressed in clown costumes. But what I believe doesn't really matter. I have to go with the facts. And these are the facts. And I think you know more about this than you are letting on."

"Why do you say that?"

"This naked guy in Saskatchewan knew all about you and the incident at the farm. And you were there that afternoon on the farm. We've already established that. And even Beatrice, the owner of the farm claims she saw the same thing. Something's going on, Winters, and I think you're holding out on me."

"Sorry, but I don't have anything."

"Well, I did some checking. The naked guy also happens to be the husband of a client of yours. That's quite the coincidence, don't you think?"

I tried to shrug it off, but he had me.

"And those gashes in the wall inside, in parallel groups of three, are suspiciously similar to the gashes in your walls when your place got wrecked last year. You know what I think?"

"No, but I have a feeling you're about to tell me."

"I don't like coincidences, Winters. And there's way too many here. I think the same guys that came after you last year came here for Johnnie, and I think you know more than you're telling me."

"You don't think I could possibly have anything to do with my own son's kidnapping," I said, anger heating up my words.

"No, I don't. But that doesn't mean you don't know something about who did it."

I shrugged my shoulders. "Sorry Detective, I don't know anything. Believe me, I'd tell you if I did."

He held out his hand. "You're a lousy liar, Winters. Maybe that's one of the things I've always liked about you. Let's see your phone."

"Why?"

"Gilda said you had pictures on it of the...whatever it was that took Johnnie."

I was cornered. "Don't you need a warrant or something?"

"Technically, yeah. But if you've got nothing to hide, why not help me out?"

I shook my head. "No can do," I said. "It's a matter of principle. I can't allow my personal rights and freedoms to be trampled on. If we start to allow that, then before you know it we'll be living in a police state."

I started to walk away. All I wanted to do was get away from Wolfowitz and start looking for Johnnie. The police couldn't help me with this. I'd start with Gluplock and Xunathnick. If anyone could help me hunt down the aliens, they could.

But Wolfowitz wasn't going to be put off that easy. He grabbed my arm. "Not so fast, Winters. You're coming with me."

I pulled my arm away. "I'm not going anywhere with you. I'm going to find my son, and I can't do that wasting my time with you."

But he grabbed my arm and twisted it, trying to get me to turn so he could get cuffs on me. I broke free and ran for the gate, hoping to get through it and into the back alley.

Wolfowitz shouted, but I didn't stop. I was pretty sure I could outrun the beefy Wolfowitz.

But I couldn't outrun the uniformed cop waiting for me at the gate. He came through it when Wolfowitz shouted, and I ran right into him. The two cops wrestled me to the ground and pulled my arms behind my back. Wolfowitz pushed my face into the dirt and got cuffs on me. "You're under arrest, Winters."

"What for?"

"I'll think of something." He patted me down while the other cop kept a knee on my back. Wolfowitz found my phone. "Now, let's see those pictures," he said. He was silent for a minute. I couldn't see what he was doing, being face down in the dirt, but apparently he found what he was looking for.

He let out a long slow whistle. "Holy crap, that thing is ugly."

Then he said: "Jack Winters, you are under arrest for withholding evidence and obstruction of justice. That's good enough for now. I'll think of more on our way down to the station."

I looked up at the porch as the cops hauled me to my feet. Gilda stood there, looking down at me with a self-satisfied smirk on her face.

CHAPTER TWO

"WHY ARE YOU HARASSING me instead of looking for Johnnie?" I shouted. "You're wasting time!"

Wolfowitz and another plain-clothes cop sat across the table from me in the small interview room, looking at me much like you might look at a bug under glass.

My wrists were cuffed to the chair behind my back. Photographs of the scene at Gilda's house covered the surface of the table in front of us. My phone also sat on the table. They'd printed some of the pictures from my phone and they were spread out across the table along with the photos from Gilda's.

The pictures from my phone were the ones I'd taken on Carimeth and Donna's farm after the incident last year with the alien bounty-hunters. Fortunately it was so far beyond their experience they didn't know what to make of it, and hadn't even come close to guessing the truth, which worked out well for me. Trying to explain those pictures to an uninitiated Earthling could prove to be just a little awkward.

I pulled at the cuffs in frustration. I was the only one with a chance of finding my son – mostly because, as Wolfowitz rightly suspected – I knew who'd taken him. But I couldn't do anything while trapped here in the police station.

"Relax Winters," Wolfowitz said. "Pulling at the cuffs doesn't do any good."

"How can I relax when my son has been taken?"

"Why don't you start by telling us what you know?"

"I can't tell you anything."

Seriously, what was I going to do? Tell them about my trip into space, the firefight on a distant planet called Carimeth in which I helped kill an alien bounty hunter that had been intent on killing me and my friends? Friends, who by the way, were also alien — but the nice kind.

I needed to get away and contact Gluplock and Xunathnick so we could start looking.

"The pictures on the phone would suggest otherwise," the other cop said.

"They're just pictures of a friend dressed in a monster costume, that's all. It has nothing to do with Johnnie."

"I don't buy it Winters. According to your ex, these friends in monster costumes also wreaked her place and took Johnnie. So who are these friends?"

"We're wasting our time in here. The bad guys are getting away with Johnnie."

Wolfowitz leaned back in his chair. "First, we don't know where to start looking. So there's not much we can do but wait for the kidnappers to contact Gilda and make their demands known. I've got officers over there with her now, waiting for the call."

Then he tapped a finger on a photograph of the wall with the strange writing. "Second, that writing on the wall might tell us something. I've got linguistics experts working on the translation, but so far they haven't even been able to figure out what language it is. But they are certain its some kind of writing. Do you know what country the kidnappers are from?"

Not country. Planet. But that wasn't a detail I could share. I shook my head.

He regarded me coolly. "Now, I've been helpful and told you what I know. But I get the feeling you're holding out on me. Why don't you tell me what you know? It may help us find Johnnie faster."

"If there was anything I could do to help, I would."

Wolfowitz stood up, anger flashing across his face. "I'm losing patience with you. Your son's been kidnapped, and you know something about it. I don't have any use for guys who..."

He suddenly stopped in mid-sentence, mouth wide open as if to say more, but nothing came. I waited for him to finish. At first I thought something had surprised him. His eyes continued to glare at me, but he didn't move. He remained utterly still.

"Wolfowitz?" I said.

When he didn't respond I looked over at his partner. He wasn't moving either, completely immobile in his chair. Not a muscle moved on his face while he looked straight at me.

"Wolfowitz?" I said looking from one to the other. "Guys, what gives?"

No response. Not a muscle moved.

Just then the door to the interview room flung open and in walked the little elfin guy from my office.

"Ah, I see I've arrived in the nick of time," he said bowing towards me. "Montclair to the rescue, sir."

I looked at Montclair, then at the two immobilised cops and back at Montclair. "What's going on?"

"I'm here to rescue you, of course. Now, let's see about releasing you from those chains." He went over to Wolfowitz and began to search his pockets. The little guy barely reached Wolfowitz's chest. The entire time Montclair rummaged through his pockets Wolfowitz didn't move.

"Montclair, what did you do?" It didn't take a rocket scientist to connect the dots.

"Oh, not to worry. They've been immobilized by a stasis field. Completely harmless. They'll be fine in a few minutes, but we must hurry. We don't want to be here when it wears off."

Not finding what he wanted, he went to the second cop and searched pockets. A moment later I heard keys rattling. "Ah, I believe I've found what we need," Montclair said. He turned to face me, holding a key chain up and rattled it for emphasis.

"Montclair, the other cops? This building is full of them. We'll never get out of here."

"Not to worry, old boy. They've all been immobilised, like our two friends here. We'll be able to leave unmolested."

"How did you do that?"

He pulled back his leather tunic to reveal belts around his waist and across his chest. The belts held several small pouches, a few knives, and what looked like a pistol. He pointed to a bluish-green metal box with a touch screen and buttons. "This instrument here has many useful functions," he said.

He held the keys up. "Now, back to the urgent matter at hand. I believe one of these keys will release you."

I pulled at the cuffs holding my arms behind the back of the chair. "Great. Get these cuffs off and we can get out of here."

Montclair continued to hold them up but didn't make a move towards me. "Let's not be so hasty. We have something to discuss first."

I frowned. "We can talk after we get out of here."

A gleam came into his eyes. "Not until you agree to my proposition."

"What? You're going to bargain with me now?"

"Of course. What better time! Before I release you, I'd like you to reconsider my offer of employment."

"And if I refuse?"

He pursed his lips and said: "That would be unfortunate. I'd have no choice but to leave you here."

I yanked violently at the chains, wanting to reach his scrawny little throat, but the chains pulled me up short. "Listen, you little pipsqueak. My son's been kidnapped. I need to get out of here and go find him."

"Then the sooner we come to terms, the better for us all."

I glared at him. "Do you know anything about the creatures that have stolen my son?"

"Of course. I've travelled a bit around the galaxy and have had the misfortune of running into the foul Rajnack."

"Then you know about the danger my son is in. I don't even know if he is alive. How can you stand there and blackmail me like this?"

"Oh, your son is very much alive, rest assured."

"How do you know that?"

He went to the other side of the table, stood next to the immobile Wolfowitz and placed a hand on one of the photographs from Gilda's. It was a photograph of the writing on the wall. "Because of the message those monsters left on the wall."

"You can read it?"

"Yes, I'm fluent in fourteen different languages."

"What does it say?"

"All in good time. Now, about my proposal. What do you say, eh? Shall we team up?"

"About the only thing I hate more than being blackmailed is going into space. Not after what happened last time."

"You don't have much choice. If you want to find your son, you will need to go into space, I'm afraid."

"You know where they've taken Johnnie?"

He looked down at the photograph. "Yes, I think I do."

"Then take me there."

"Only after you agree to help me."

"This is blackmail. You're taking advantage of my situation to blackmail me while I'm helpless."

He knotted his bushy eyebrows together. "Oh, I wouldn't put it in such a crude manner. I'm merely using the leverage at hand to encourage a mutually beneficial arrangement."

"Forget it. I will just call Gluplock. He'll help me."

"And how will you do that from jail? And it will take them some time to get here, even if you did manage to contact them. Several weeks, if not months. Space is a big place, after all. Can you really afford to lose that much time?"

He had a good point, and I began to see that I didn't have much of a choice. Either go with Montclair now, and have a chance at finding Johnnie, or sit here in chains.

But Montclair wanted something too, and badly. Badly enough to come to Earth to see me, and then find me here at the police station. That gave me some leverage as well.

"Okay, but you can't possibly expect me to go looking for a missing brooch while my son is being held captive by the Rajnack."

"So we are both in a bind. What do you propose?"

"Help me get Johnnie first, then I will help you find your missing jewelry. Once Johnnie is safe, I'll go wherever you need me."

"Do you swear on your honour?"

"Yes, I'll even sign a contract if you want."

He came around the table to me and stuck out a hand. "No contract is necessary. A handshake will suffice."

I pulled at the cuffs holding my arms behind the chair. "I can't really shake on it right now. Will a promise do?"

"Oh, of course. Silly of me. Is your word your bond?"

"Yes. I always keep my promises."

"Then I am satisfied. You strike me as a man of honour. The Radauti would never have recommended you otherwise."

Montclair stepped around behind me, and I could feel him trying various keys in the lock of my cuffs. The entire time I looked at Wolfowitz, who just looked back at me unmoving. After what seemed like an eternity, one of the keys worked and the cuffs fell free.

I stood up and rubbed at my wrists. "Thanks, I think."

"You are to be congratulated, sir. You drive a hard bargain. Now, let's go get your young Johnnie."

I grabbed my phone off the table. Montclair picked up the photograph of the message on the wall and folded it into an inner pocket. "We'll need this for reference," he said.

I looked around the room. "I need to find my wallet and keys. They were taken from me and must be here somewhere."

"That will take time we can ill afford. Where we are going you'll have no need of them. We must make all haste. Hurry now!"

Montclair was first to the door, opened it and went out. I followed him down a hall into a large room filled with desks and chairs. Uniformed police stood around the room like mannequins frozen in mid-stride, or sitting at desks, captured in a moment of time.

Only one person moved. Donna walked slowly around the frozen cops, looking quizzically at them, as she made her way across the room towards us.

"Donna," I shouted.

She had on tight fitting blue jeans, knee high brown leather boots and a black leather jacket. She wore a white toque. Her shoulder length brown hair hung loose. "Jack! What's going on?"

I went over to her. "What are you doing here?"

She looked around the room full of immobilized cops. "I heard you'd been arrested. Why is everyone in the building frozen?"

"Montclair did it. Do you have your car with you?"

"Yes. Who's Montclair?" Then she spotted Montclair, standing a few feet back. "Who's the little guy in the elf costume?"

Montclair's back stiffened and he glared at Donna. "I am neither an elf, nor am I little. While it is true that my race is shorter than yours, on my world I am not short."

"Donna, meet Montclair."

She raised an eyebrow. "He looks like an elf."

"Guys, we don't have time for this," I said. "We need to get going."

But Donna didn't move. She crossed her arms and stared at me with frost in her eyes. "I'm not going anywhere without an explanation. I came down here to bail you out, and instead I find you with what appears to be an elf in a steampunk costume and all the police frozen. What's going on?"

Montclair bristled with indignation. "I am not an *elf*," he sputtered. "Please desist from calling me an elf!"

"Johnnie's been kidnapped," I said quietly.

Her eyes widened with horror and she covered her mouth with a hand. "Oh my God, Jack."

"Do you remember those aliens that attacked us on your mother's farm last year?"

She nodded. "How could I ever forget?"

"More of them came back today and got Johnnie."

Her eyes watered up. "Poor Johnnie. This is awful. What are we going to do?"

"Go find him," I said with steel in my voice.

"How?"

"I haven't had time to figure that part out yet. But there are options. Montclair here seems to have some idea where they went."

"Jack," Donna said softly. "The Rajnack are ruthless monsters. I hate to ask, but, how do you know he's…" she stopped, hating to finish the thought, but I knew what she was asking. It was a fair question.

"I don't know Donna," my voice cracked. "But I have to proceed on the assumption he is still alive."

Montclair stepped forward. "I believe I can be of assistance with that question. I went to Gilda's looking for Jack and I saw the note the Rajnack left on the wall, which I am able to read – mostly. Parts of it still require some translation work. But we must get away from here before the stasis field holding the police wears off."

"Hey, where'd you guys come from?" A surprised voice called.

I turned around. One of the police mannequins had returned to life, and was staring right at us, eyes wide and mouth open in surprise. Cops around the room slowly stirred to life, as if awaking from a long sleep.

"Too late," Montclair whispered. "We'd better run."

"Can't you just reactivate it?" I asked.

"No," he said and started walking quickly for the door.

"Hey stop them!" Wolfowitz bellowed from the hall.

I grabbed Donna's arm and we bolted for the door, quickly passing Montclair. When we reached the door I looked back, expecting to see a dozen cops bearing down on us. But Wolfowitz had barely moved, walking slowly and stiffly. Other cops were trying to follow us, but could only manage slow, stiff walks. Some even dragged a leg, zombie style.

Montclair reached us at the door. "What's wrong with them?" I asked.

"They are still stiff from the effects of the stasis field. It will be another hour or so before they are completely thawed out and back to normal. But I wouldn't dally."

"Winters, stop, you're under arrest," Wolfowitz yelled.

"Sorry, Wolfie. I'd love to stay and chat, but I need to go find my son." Then the three of us walked quickly out the front door.

CHAPTER THREE

WE JUMPED INTO DONNA'S PRIUS. She got behind the wheel, I got into the front seat and Montclair took the back. Donna pushed the start button. "Where to?"

"Back to my place," I said.

Donna watched for an opening and pulled out into traffic, talking the entire time. "No Jack. That's the first place the cops are going to watch."

"They're still feeling the effects of the stasis field. If we're quick, we should be all right. I need to get my Radauti timepiece and another gun."

"And how did you freeze a room full of cops?"

I shrugged. "Don't ask me. That was Montclair's handiwork."

"The dwarf?" She twisted around to look into the backseat. "The little guy did that?"

"Can you just drive," I said. "We can explain everything later."

Montclair exhaled. "I am not a dwarf either, madam. Not an elf nor a dwarf. Please desist from calling me either one."

She looked at him in the rear-view mirror. "So where are you from?"

"A charming little planet not too far from here. Thirty odd light-years, give or take."

"An alien? Seriously?"

"If by alien you mean that I am not indigenous to your planet, then yes, I am an alien."

"You're a bit short to be an alien, aren't you?"

Montclair bristled. "I'm not short where I come from."

"Not all aliens are eight feet tall, Donna," I said. The only other aliens Donna had met were my Radauti friends, Gluplock and Xunathnick, and the Rajnack bounty hunters. Radauti typically grew to over eight feet tall but were very slim. The Rajnack were almost as tall but much bigger, with massive chests and forearms.

"So why didn't you use that thingy on them again, what did you call it?" Donna asked.

"Stasis field," Montclair said.

"Yeah, whatever. Why didn't you just use that thingy again when they started to wake up?"

"Using it on them again this soon could cause permanent damage or even death," he said. "I didn't want to risk it."

"Why didn't your stasis gizmo freeze Jack too?"

"The device has some very sophisticated controls that allows me to be selective in its range and effect. So, for this exercise I set it to immobilize everyone in the building except Jack."

"So then why wasn't I frozen?"

"You weren't in the building when I used it. You came along after, correct?"

Donna nodded. "And you just happened to be down at the cop shop...why?"

Donna's attention was a bit too distracted for my comfort, split as it was between the road, her never ending questions, and looking in the rear-view at Montclair. It all added up to make me a very nervous passenger.

"Donna," I snapped. "Can you hold back your inexhaustible curiosity until we are some place safe, and just focus on the road, please!"

They both ignored my little outburst. Montclair said: "I went there to effect Jack's rescue, of course".

She looked sideways at me as she drove. "If Johnnie has been kidnapped, why did they arrest you?"

I let out a long, slow breath. "Wolfowitz suspected I knew more than I was telling, which of course is true, so he arrested me for withholding evidence and obstruction."

Traffic was heavy and Donna started to weave around slower moving cars. "So why didn't you tell the cops what you know? We need all the help we can get finding Johnnie."

Donna was nothing if not curious. And she always had a follow-up question. I was starting to feel like I was back at the cop shop in the interrogation room. "Come on Donna. Get real. What was I supposed to tell them? Aliens had taken Johnnie?"

"Point taken."

That seemed to satisfy her curiosity, for the moment anyway. She drove in silence for a few minutes. But something occurred to me and I turned around in my seat to face Montclair. He was concentrating on a photograph in his hands. His legs dangled from the seat.

"So why did you happen to be down at the police station? How did you know to find me there?" I asked.

He looked up from the photograph. "As I told the female, to rescue you."

"Sure, but how did you find me?"

"If he calls me female one more time," Donna snapped, "I'm going to stop the car and throw him out."

"I followed you down to your ex-female's home. Gilda, I believe her name was."

"You followed me?"

'Yes. I was hoping to resume our little chat about your employment. When I arrived, Gilda told me you had been arrested. She seemed rather pleased by it, too, if I am able to read human facial expression accurately."

"I think you probably read it very accurately," I said.

"Once I knew you'd been arrested, it wasn't hard to find the address of the police station."

"Ex-female?" Donna hissed. "What kind of sexist, Neanderthal, backwater planet do you come from?"

I addressed Montclair without looking at her. "You mentioned something about being able to read the message on the wall? Can you do that?"

"If you will give me a moment, I'm translating it now."

"What message?" Donna shouted as she yanked the steering wheel to the left. The car veered into another lane around a slow truck. Montclair tilted in the back seat and almost fell over.

"Madam, your driving is making my job much more difficult than it needs to be," Montclair said.

"Donna, would you slow down. You're going to attract attention driving like this," I said.

She ignored us. "What about the message?"

"The Rajnack left a message written on the wall at Gilda's. Montclair is translating it now."

"I didn't think those monsters could write," Donna said.

"Of course they have language," Montclair said. "They may be brutal, but they are nonetheless intelligent and capable of interstellar flight."

"You can read it?" I asked.

He sighed. A very human sounding sigh of exasperation. "I could if the both of you would stop asking so many questions and allow me to concentrate."

Donna braked hard, almost slamming me into the dashboard. Montclair pitched forward and fell off the seat. We were in front of my townhouse. "Be quick Jack. We don't have long."

Montclair was sputtering indignation and climbing back onto the seat as I opened the door. "Keep the engine running," I yelled.

Wolfowitz had taken my keys, phone, wallet and gun when I was arrested. I kept a spare key hidden under the front porch. I wouldn't need my bank cards and ID where I was going, but I wanted a gun and my Radauti timepiece. I retrieved the key from under the porch and let myself in.

It had only been that morning when I was last home, but with the events of the day it felt like a year. I ran down into the basement, jumping two or three steps at a time.

With the money I made selling coffee to aliens I was able to completely renovate. Heck, with the money I made, I could have paid cash for a mansion, with an indoor pool, circular front driveway and snobby butlers with fake English accents.

But I wasn't the conspicuous consumer type and needed to keep a low profile anyway, so I stayed in my humble two-bedroom townhouse.

However, as a reward to myself I had converted the basement into a very comfortable man-cave. It had a bar, cooler stocked with beer, huge leather couch, fireplace, gun rack, and an eighty-inch flat screen TV that got seven hundred and sixty-three channels. That's not including the Wi-Fi and Android box.

The best place in the world to watch football and hockey.

I grabbed an end of the couch and swung it to the side, then rolled back the area rug to reveal the safe I'd installed in the cement floor. The safe had a biometric lock. I pressed my finger onto the pad and heard the bolts release. I opened the door and took out a Ruger Blackhawk 44, ammo and the Radauti timepiece.

I strapped the timepiece onto my wrist. Gluplock had given it to me last year, after the Rajnack had attacked us at Donna's farm and almost killed everyone in the world I care most about. Gluplock said I could use the timepiece to protect myself from the Rajnack if they ever came back.

Well, they were back.

I closed the safe, replaced the rug and the couch. I kept a shoulder harness hanging from a peg under my rifle rack and strapped it on. I looked at the rifle rack and grabbed the Winchester 30-30 and a Mossberg semi-automatic. Then for good measure I grabbed the Benelli 12-gauge pump action shotgun.

It wouldn't do to go looking for the Rajnack without proper weaponry. It would be suicidal, as a matter of fact.

I went to my gun locker, grabbed extra ammo, and stuffed it into a backpack. Then I went back out the front door and locked up the house, pocketed the key and walked quickly back to the car. I tossed the guns and ammo in the trunk and got into the front seat next to Donna.

"Did you get it?" Donna asked. I buckled up as she stepped on the gas. Then I held up my wrist to display the timepiece. It looked like a huge oversized square watch or small tablet.

I turned to Montclair in the back. He looked pleased with himself. "Any luck with the translation?" I asked.

"Yes, and I have every confidence your young son is alive."

"What does it say?"

"It's a ransom note as we suspected. The Rajnack want us to meet them tomorrow morning with the pay-off, in exchange for Johnnie."

"What do they want?" Donna asked.

"Coffee," Montclair said.

"Coffee?" She repeated.

"Yes. It's worth a fortune on the black market."

"I assume you mean the black market in space." Donna said.

"Yes, of course. Where else?" Montclair said.

"Do you think the Rajnack can be trusted? I mean, is Johnnie still...okay?" I choked.

"No," Montclair said. "They cannot be trusted. But Johnnie is fine, for now. The Rajnack are thoroughly foul and wicked creatures. But they are also very greedy, and that for now works to our advantage. They want the coffee. It will get them a small fortune, so they will keep Johnnie alive until they get what they want."

"Guys," Donna yelled. "Can we sort this out later? Right now we have more immediate problems."

She was looking in the rear-view mirror. I turned around and looked out the back. A police cruiser with flashing red lights raced up the street behind us.

"Can you outrun them?" I asked.

"In a Prius? Get real."

I had a gun, but I wasn't about to start shooting at the cops. "Montclair, any ideas?"

But Montclair was already unbuckling and turning around. He stood up on the backseat to look out. "Law enforcement officers, I believe."

"Yes."

He pulled a pistol off his belt. "If you could keep the vehicle steady for a moment, madam."

"Stop calling me madam! How old do you think I am?" Donna yelled.

"Don't shoot at them," I said.

He aimed his pistol out the back window. "Montclair, don't!" I shouted.

"Have no fear, Jack. I am not a murderer or thug. They will come to no harm," he said and pulled the trigger. It went *spiffzat*, and a sizzling noise pierced the air. Another car the police cruiser was passing suddenly slowed and veered to the side.

"Drat and bother, I missed! Please do hold this carriage steady, madam."

"I'm going to choke him as soon as we are someplace safe," Donna hissed.

He took another shot, and the cruiser began to slow suddenly. I watched it pull to the side of the road.

"What did you do?" I asked.

"My pistol has several settings. I used a focused electromagnetic pulse beam that interfered with the voltage in the electrical systems of the target. That stopped the engine and forced them to roll to a stop. No one was hurt."

"Nice," I said.

"Where to next guys?" Donna asked.

"The farm. We have a couple tons of coffee in the barn. We can use the farm truck to bring it to the rendezvous with the Rajnack," I said.

Donna nodded. "We'll need to be quick. It won't be long before the cops come around the farm asking questions."

She stomped on the gas, and we headed out of town as fast as her Prius could take us.

Which wasn't all that fast.

CHAPTER FOUR

"WHAT NOW?" Donna asked. The three of us sat in the cab of Beatrice's farm truck, engine and heater running to keep warm. The headlights of the truck shone out across a dark field, empty except for a few stubs of corn stalk poking up through the snow, illuminated by our lights.

The Rajnack had chosen the site well. The field was surrounded by thick woods, hidden from the nearest road by an abandoned warehouse and trees.

"We wait," I said. I checked my watch. Still two hours before sunrise. "It shouldn't be long, if our friends are punctual."

"I strongly disagree with this, Jack," Montclair said, not for the first time. "I wish you'd reconsider."

"I'm not going to play games with these monsters and risk irritating them. It will only put Johnnie at more risk."

"We should have stayed with my plan. You don't understand them the way I do," he said. "I'm afraid they will just take the coffee and keep Johnnie."

"You said yourself they wanted the coffee, not Johnnie."

"Yes, but now with all the coffee here, you have no leverage to force them to release Johnnie. If you'd just listened to me, I believe our chances of getting Johnnie back are greater."

"If I'd listened to you, we would have met them here without the ransom, hidden the coffee at another location, and demanded they release Johnnie before telling them where the coffee was."

"Yes."

"And risk angering them? Showing up here without the coffee might have just aggravated them enough to kill Johnnie."

"I don't believe it would have gone that way. I told you already, they want the product. Greed is the only thing that will temper a Rajnack's blood thirst for revenge and violence. Holding back on the coffee was our only leverage. Now we have none."

"It's a risk either way. Johnnie is my son, so we do it my way. I think it's the safest."

"Very well. I hope this goes well, for all our sakes."

I patted the Ruger strapped to my shoulder. "I've taken out a couple of Rajnack before. I can take out another one if need be. How many settings does that pistol of yours have?"

"Everything from stun to lethal," he said.

"Just be ready with it." I checked my watch. "It's almost time. Donna, you'd better get into position."

She climbed out of the cab and walked around to the front of the truck. I got out and joined her. She held the Winchester 30-30 expertly cradled in her arms. No one was a better shot than Donna.

"Are you sure about this?" I asked.

She pulled the bolt back on the rifle with a click. "Jack, we've already been over this. Besides, I'm a better shot then you are." She added with a grin.

"True, but if anything happens to you…"

She placed a finger over my mouth. "We have to get Johnnie back, and you both have a better chance of getting out of this alive with my help. I'll be well hidden. If the exchange starts to go south, get down. Monty and I will take down the bad guys."

"Actually, when it comes to the Rajnack, the bandits aren't guys. They're all female. The males stay home. Don't be such a sexist."

"Hmm, they're not all that stupid then," she grinned. "Maybe they're more advanced than we give them credit for."

I held her shoulders and looked into her eyes. They sparkled back at me, telling me everything that needed to be said.

"I love you," I said.

She smiled, and my heart soared. "I know," she said.

"If anything happens to you, I'll never forgive myself. Stay out of sight, no matter what happens."

"Shush, I'll be fine. Johnnie is like a son to me, you know that. What kind of girl would I be if I let you face alien monsters alone?"

"There's starting to be a bit too many aliens around for my comfort. We have plenty of money. We'll take our money and move someplace far away. Find some nice tropical island. Avoid all alien contact."

"Move in together? Jack Winters, are you propositioning me?"

"No, I would never suggest something that would offend the sensibilities of a nice Baptist girl. Besides, I've seen your mom in action with a shotgun. Last thing I need is for her to come gunning for me. So, what I have in mind is a much more formal arrangement."

She raised her eyebrows and grinned. "Yes?"

"Donna, will you…"

Montclair shouting from the cab ruined the moment. "We have company!"

He stuck his head out the window and pointed up. Donna and I looked. An array of lights directly over the field were descending rapidly.

"This is it!" I said. "Get into the trees."

She stood on her tip toes and kissed me. "I love you. Don't get yourself killed, okay?"

"Promise. Now get going."

Donna disappeared into the trees. I felt better knowing she had my back. Montclair turned off the lights and jumped from the truck. Together we walked out into the field and stopped about twenty feet in front of the truck.

We stood a few feet apart, not too close, but close enough that Montclair could translate for me. I didn't know Rajnack, and I couldn't be sure they'd speak English.

We looked up and waited. A dark object descended slowly from the sky towards me, blocking out the stars overheard. I swallowed a lump in my throat and fought to keep my screaming nerves steady.

I thought about Johnnie, up in that ship, wondering what terrors he'd been through, and the hot glow of anger expanding in my chest overcame the natural fear of coming face to face with monsters in the dark.

I'd faced these creatures before. *You can do this, Jack,* I told myself. *Stay steady. This is for Johnnie.*

The silver ship landed softly on the ground, nose towards me, maybe a hundred feet away. Long, sleek, and with wings, its aerodynamic design was clearly meant for flying within an atmosphere, not just the vacuum of space.

Not that I'm a NASA nerd or anything, but I'd learned a thing or two during my travels with my alien friends. It certainly didn't look anything like the Rajnack ship that had landed behind Beatrice's farm the previous year.

Lights from the front of the ship snapped on, illuminating us and the surrounding field. I'd never felt so naked and exposed. A ramp lowered to the ground from the ship's undercarriage, and a large shadow appeared at the top.

"Ready with that pistol of yours?" I whispered to Montclair.

He grunted and gave his pocket a pat.

A hulking shape made its way down the ramp and stopped at the bottom. It was at least seven feet tall, almost as tall as a Radauti, but with a huge bulky figure, thick chest and massive forearms that almost reached the ground. It stood upright on proportionately smaller legs. There was no neck to speak of. Its massive shoulders just sloped up to its head.

It wore a tight-fitting silver suit and large three toed boots. Its head was exposed, so they must be used to an atmosphere roughly similar to ours, but it had a tube running into its nose from a small pack on its back.

This was the first time I'd ever faced a Rajnack that wasn't shooting at me. I'd forgotten just how ugly they were. And these were the females.

It took a couple steps forward and looked at me with small eyes darker than coal. I didn't move, wanting it to come closer so

Donna could get a better shot if things went bad. But it stayed close to the ramp and spoke in slow, halting English that sounded like a low growl.

"I see they have sent a male to do a female's work."

Hearing it speak English came as a jolt. I don't know why, but I guess I just wasn't expecting that. It took me a moment to recover from the surprise before I answered. "We try not to be gender specific in our roles," I said. "It upsets people."

It made a noise sounding something like a grunt or cough. I couldn't tell what it was supposed to mean, or if it was just sneezing.

Then it said: "You are the human who is trading with the Radauti?"

It wasn't clear to me whether it was a statement or a question. "Yes," I said.

"You will now trade with us. All your dealings with the Radauti slime will cease."

"Wow, you're really not much for small talk, are you? You just jump right to the point."

"Have you brought what we required, human?"

I gestured towards the truck behind us. "It's all there."

It made a grunting noise.

"I've done my part. Now, where's my son?"

"Your part is not completed. Until then your male offspring will remain with us."

My chest tightened with panic. "We had a deal. I've brought you the coffee. Now release my son."

"I am changing the terms of our agreement. All your trade with the Radauti will stop. You will now trade only with us. Twenty krools of coffee every half turn of your planet around its star."

What choice did I have? Gluplock and Xunathnick would understand. I could even help them find another coffee supplier. I didn't care about the money.

"Okay, sure. I'll stop trading with the Radauti and deal exclusively with you. Just release my son."

A cackling noise erupted from its throat. I supposed it was some kind of laugh or derisive chuckle. "Do you take us for simpletons? Your son will remain with us to ensure your subservience."

I stepped forward suddenly. I considered giving Donna the signal. Brush the side of my hair with my left hand, and she'd drop this animal.

But I held off. Johnnie was still in the ship, or so I assumed. If this was just a landing craft, then he may be up in the mother ship. I just didn't know. And there could be more of these critters inside.

"You can't do this!" I shouted. But I could see it was like trying to reason with an animal, something with no moral sense.

"Why do you make blatant statements of nonsense, human? Of course I can do this. If I have the power to do it, then it is my right. You will comply or I will crush your offspring's head and leave his corpse on your doorstep."

A rage kindled inside me that I'd never felt before. Keeping myself under control came as a monumental struggle that I wasn't sure I could win. Do I start a firefight, with a good chance I'll get myself and Montclair killed?

I kept my voice low and even. "For how long? How long will you keep my child?"

"For as long as we require. As long as you comply, your offspring lives. Disobey, and it dies."

They were going to keep him indefinitely! With those final words, my anger got the better of me. This could go on forever. How long could Johnnie live under the conditions they were keeping him? His chances of long-term survival were better if I rushed the ship and rescued him now.

The three of us had memorized several plans covering all the scenarios and contingencies that we could imagine. It took me all of a split second to make the decision.

I started to raise my hand to signal Donna when Montclair suddenly stepped forward, grabbed my arm to restrain me, and spoke to the Rajnack in a strange language I'd never heard before.

The monster in front of me waited for Montclair to finish before growling something in response in the same language. Then it turned around and went up the ramp into the ship.

Montclair kept his hand on my arm until the Rajnack was no longer in sight and the ramp closed.

"Why did you stop me from signalling Donna?" I asked.

"Because you would have only succeeded in getting us all killed. And probably get Johnnie killed too, since once you're dead they have no further use for him."

"Why do you think that?"

"You may not have noticed because you were pre-occupied with the Rajnack, but several of the ship's protrusions are weapons, and they are aimed at us. Also, the craft is large, large enough for an interstellar light-drive. It's possible this is the mothership itself, not just a landing craft. As such, it would have a large crew. I estimate there could be as many as ten or more of those creatures inside."

That sobered me up a bit. And if I had got myself killed, where would that leave Johnnie? And what would have happened to Donna?

"What did you say to it?"

"I told it that we will be their humble and obedient servants, and comply with their demands."

I wanted to choke him. I turned on him in a rage, fighting the temptation to pull out my Ruger. "Did you hear what it said? They're going to keep Johnnie. If I don't do something, I'll never see him again."

"And if you'd given into your impulse to start shooting, you'd certainly never see him again because you'd be dead. Along with Donna and myself, I might add."

"Why did you tell the Rajnack that?"

"To buy us time to think of a good plan, something that isn't as suicidal as what you were about to do. Stop and think about it, Jack. We are not without resources. We have powerful allies in the Radauti."

We were still in front of the ship, which hadn't moved. "What now?" I asked.

"We walk away, leaving the truck here. They will load the coffee and be back in six months for more."

"I can't just supply them with coffee indefinitely while they keep Johnnie."

"Of course not," he said.

"There must be something we can do. We have to think of something."

"And that's exactly what we will do as soon as we are away from here," he said.

∞

The three of us made the long walk back through the woods. It was still an hour before sunrise, and we had to use flashlights to pick our way through the tangled undergrowth and tree roots.

We walked in silence, too heavy of heart to speak. At one point I glanced back and saw at least a half dozen Rajnack on the ground around their ship.

We found Donna's Prius where we left it, hidden behind the warehouse out of sight from the main road, and gathered next to it, not sure where to go.

No one spoke for several long minutes. Finally, Montclair broke the heavy silence. "They'll be back in six months, they said. They want the coffee, so we can be fairly confident they will return. That will give us plenty of time to plan a rescue. And your Radauti friends can be here by then to assist."

I shook my head. "That leaves Johnnie with them for too long. I don't want to think about the horrors he will go through. We need to get him back sooner."

"You are a Friend of the Radauti. Can you contact them?" Montclair asked.

"That's not a bad idea, dear," Donna said. "Why don't you call Gluplock for help?"

"I'm not expecting them for another two months. I can use my timepiece to send them a message, but it will take weeks for it to reach them. By then, it will be too late. The Rajnack will be long gone."

Montclair rubbed the whiskers on his chin. "He's right, that's not nearly fast enough. We need to follow them while their ion trail is still fresh. We'll just have to pursue the Rajnack ourselves, without any help. But we must be quick."

"Follow the Rajnack into space?" Donna asked.

"Of course."

"How do you plan on doing that?" I asked.

"In my spaceship of course! I have a perfectly serviceable one. It will be a bit cramped with the three of us, but we'll manage."

Chapter Five

I PINCHED THE BRIDGE OF MY NOSE. "Okay, so let me just recap. The plan is we follow the Rajnack into space, and hope for an opportunity to rescue Johnnie. And we have to do this on our own, because the Radauti can't get here soon enough. Is that about it?"

Donna nodded. "Yup."

"That sounds like a reasonable summation," Montclair said.

"Okay, well, it's crazy," I said. "But I don't see any other way. We can't leave Johnnie with them for six months. We have to follow the aliens now and get him back."

Montclair stroked his chin. "And we have our agreement, Jack. My spaceship is at your service."

I turned to Donna. "This is going to be very dangerous," I said. "I'll understand if you don't come."

She grinned. "And let you have all the fun? No way. I'm in. Besides, Johnnie is like a son to me."

"Okay, let's do this," I said.

"Then it's decided," Montclair said. "But we need to be quick, while the ion trail left by the Rajnack ship is still fresh."

We were going to be in space for several weeks, possibly months, and would need supplies. We made a quick stop at a grocery store, then headed for Monty's ship. Everything had to be non-perishable, so we crammed the car with canned food and bags of jerky, dried fruits and nuts.

Fortunately, Montclair could eat the same food we could. I was surprised at how similar to humans he was, but when I asked him about that he dodged the question. I made a mental note to follow-up on that later, but for now we had a spaceship to provision.

∞

It was close to noon when Donna pulled over to the side of a country road next to thick woods. Montclair pointed at the woods. "My ship is in there."

I looked around. There were no signs of humanity in sight. "We should be fine here for a while," I said. "Let's be quick."

We got out of the car and trudged through the snow-covered woods. About thirty minutes later we reached a small meadow. Tall blades of dead brown grass poked up through the snow.

The meadow was open to the sky and a large brass bullet-shaped object with wings sat in the middle of it. It narrowed at the front to a rounded point, and the back was flat. There were round port holes down the side, and a large window just above the front tip. An inch of snow covered the wings.

"Well, what do you think? She's a beauty, isn't she? She's been in the family for generations," Montclair said.

"You mean it's old?" Donna asked.

"I would say *well broken in* and *proven reliable over time*. One never knows what to expect with a new ship. But I know what this ship can do. You can count on her."

Montclair walked ahead of us. Donna muttered, "Great. We're going into space in his grandfather's spaceship. I don't care what he says, if I was going on a long drive, I'd prefer a new car, not Grandpa's Model T."

"You're over thinking things. Come on, its not like we have many options."

We followed Montclair and walked up to the ship, ducked under the wings, and came to a door in the side. The craft stood about three feet off the ground on legs.

Montclair flipped open a small access panel to reveal a keypad and punched at it with an index finger. The door slid open, and a short stepladder extended to the ground.

"The door requires a code. We can go over that and various other things you'll need to know later, once we're underway." Then he climbed up the ladder and disappeared into the doorway. Donna and I looked at each other and then followed him inside.

The interior was dark but light from the door and portholes allowed us to see our surroundings. If the Byzantines had built submarines, then I imagined they might have looked something like the inside of Montclair's ship.

We'd both been in spaceships before, but our experience had only been with Radauti built craft. In sharp contrast to the open and airy interior of Radauti ships, Montclair's was small and cramped.

We stood in a passageway running the length of the ship, and had to bend over to keep from hitting our heads on the brass conduit running along the ceiling. There was lots of brass, leather padding and dark wood panelling.

To our left the passageway led to what appeared to be the cockpit. I could see Montclair inside getting settled into a chair. Donna and I went down the long passageway, heads ducked low, and entered the cockpit.

More leather and brass. The cockpit had four seats. Two facing the windows to the front, and another two behind them. The arms of the chairs had built in controls, and most of the surfaces were covered in dark screens, panels, brass buttons and toggle switches.

Montclair sat in one of the chairs flipping switches. The control panel in front of him came to life with multi-coloured lights, and lights came on inside the ship. He flipped more switches, pressed buttons, and more lights and screens came to life.

"Heat should be on in a moment. Still a bit frosty in here I'm afraid. But we should be up and running in a few minutes." Donna sat down in the other seat next to Montclair. It was too small for her and her knees came up to her chest. She sat looking around, open mouthed.

I decided to explore, turned to go, and hit my head on the top of the doorway. I bent lower and headed down the corridor rubbing my head.

I could hear Donna and Montclair talking in the cockpit behind me. I passed several doors and at one point passed through some sort of lounge, like first class seating on a jumbo jet. There were couches, soft leather chairs and tables next to screens and port holes. Brass and leather everywhere.

I opened some of the doors out of curiosity. A bit nosey, perhaps, but I was on a spaceship after all. Who wouldn't be?

Some of the other rooms looked like staterooms, with small Elf sized beds and closets. One room was clearly a toilet facility. Another room was filled with screens, keypads and dials. At the back of the ship I found a kitchen galley with lots of comfortable seating.

The ship started to hum and vibrate, coming to life all around me. It felt warmer and I could no longer see my breath. Then the floor suddenly tilted under my feet, and I put out a hand to steady myself against the bulkhead. Through a porthole I saw trees passing by below.

I went back out into the passageway and looked towards the front of the ship. The door to the cockpit was still open and I could see Monty at the controls.

"Montclair! A little warning would be nice." I shouted to be heard down the long passageway over the hum of the ship.

He twisted in his seat to look back at me over his shoulder. "Sorry Jack."

I made my way to the ship's entrance hatch, still wide open. We were flying just above the treetops. I held on to a handgrip and watched the snow-covered trees pass below.

We flew over a dirt road and Donna's Prius came into view below as Montclair spun the ship around. He set us down on the road next to the car.

Montclair and Donna unbuckled from their seats and came down the corridor to me. "Let's be quick," Montclair said.

Donna and I jumped out and together we started hauling supplies out of the car and shoving them through the ship's door, as fast as we could while keeping an eye on the road. Montclair stayed in the ship and moved stuff away from the door as we shoved stuff in.

But we weren't nearly quick enough. We only had about half the supplies transferred to the ship when movement down the road caught my eye.

A large Ford pickup raced towards us. "We've got company," I said.

Donna ran back to the car. "There's just one more bag I need," she said and started rummaging through the backseat.

"Just grab something and let's go."

"I can't find it," she said, then went to the trunk. "I know I left it here somewhere."

Monty appeared in the open door. "Please make all haste and board the ship," he said. "We've attracted the attention of the locals."

I shoved the carton of canned fruit I'd been holding through the door, and looked down the road. The pickup was still coming towards us, but slowing down.

"Donna," I yelled. "Come on."

"I can't find the toiletries," she said.

"Just leave it," I said. "We need to get out of here."

She shut the trunk and ran over to the bottom of the ladder. But instead of climbing aboard she started looking through her pockets. She found her key fob and clicked it. The lights on her car flashed.

The pickup came to a stop in front of us. The young woman behind the wheel already had a cell phone to her ear, talking into it while looking wide eyed at us.

"Will you just get in," I said.

"I wanted to lock my car. We may be gone a while," she said as she climbed up.

Montclair made his way to the cockpit. Donna squeezed by me into the passageway and followed him into the cockpit. A moment later the ship lifted slightly, tilted and then rose into the air. I stood in the open door, looking down, holding onto a handgrip. The woman in the truck held a cellphone up towards us through the windshield.

Great, I thought. In about two minutes we'll be all over YouTube and Instagram, with me clearly standing in the door of a receding spaceship.

"Montclair, the door?"

"Oh, yes. Sorry." The stepladder retracted and the door slid closed. The ship tilted up and I made my way forwards towards the front, walking up the slope of the deck towards the cockpit.

Donna sat in the seat next to Montclair. She'd found the seat adjustments and looked a lot more comfortable. I took one of the back seats. The only thing visible through the windows were grey wintery clouds.

Montclair had his hands on a joystick that came up from the floor between his legs. The instruments around him glowed and blinked with multiple colours. There were banks of brass buttons and toggle switches.

A screen in the control panel between Donna and Montclair showed the receding ground below, a patchwork of white and grey fields and farmland, crisscrossed with dark grey roads. Other screens displayed graphs and numbers.

"This is horrible," Donna said, her face knotted with worry. I could think of a lot of difficulties with our present situation, but it wasn't clear to me which of the dozens of problems we faced she referred to.

"What's that?" I asked.

"We had to leave half our stuff in the car, including clothes and other personal items."

She looked at Montclair. "How long are we going to be in space?"

"It's hard to say, but several weeks, maybe months. If it takes any longer than three or four months, we'll return to Earth and get ready for our scheduled rendezvous with the Rajnack six months hence."

"Then we have a problem. We can't spend months travelling without a change of clothes. We don't have nearly enough food and water. And I can't go more than a couple of weeks without...certain personal items."

Montclair grinned. "Are you referring to articles of feminine hygiene and grooming?"

"Yes, thank you Montclair for pointing that out."

Another problem occurred to me. "The Prius we left on the road is registered to Donna."

Donna covered her eyes with a hand. "This is going to get back to Mom. It won't take the cops long to connect the dots. Now I'm implicated. They'll be dropping by the farm to question Mom before long. As if I didn't have enough to worry about. What's Mom going to think? She'll be sick with worry."

"One problem at a time," Montclair said. "One problem at a time. Let's get Johnnie. Then we can come back and clear things up with the police."

We were gaining altitude fast. "Montclair, can we stop climbing and hover within cell range?"

He pulled the joystick back and pushed some buttons. I looked at Donna. "Put the batteries back in your phone and call your mother. It will put both your minds at ease."

"Don't be too long," Montclair said. "We don't want to attract the attention of the Air Force."

CHAPTER SIX

DONNA'S TEARS HAD DRIED BY THE TIME we reached orbit. We sat in the cockpit and watched Earth's blue and white crescent below. The eternal night of space, alive with the brilliant fire of countless stars, surrounded us.

Monty sat in his flight chair, checking instruments. The console in front of him had several curved contours to fit the round screens and instrument displays, framed in brass.

Donna still had the seat in front next to Monty, and I sat behind them looking at the instruments. I felt like a monkey staring at the console of an airliner.

"Any luck?" I asked.

"Still scanning."

Donna got up from her seat and headed down the corridor. I followed and caught up to her. She stopped and turned to look at me. We stood in the cramped corridor, slightly ducked to keep from knocking our heads against brass conduit in the ceiling. There were still boxes of supplies filling the corridor, waiting to be stowed away.

"I might start to get claustrophobic if we're stuck in here for long. Actually makes me miss the Radauti spaceship," I said. It was a poor attempt at humor that didn't help Donna's mood.

"Yeah," she said.

"Look, I feel awful about what this is putting you through. Once Monty has a lock on the Rajnack's particle trail, we can drop you off at the farm before we take off after them."

"And sit at home and wait for the police to come and arrest me for aiding a fugitive from justice?"

"Tell them I forced you."

"Even better, implicate you in another kidnapping, as if you weren't already in enough trouble." Then she added with a grin: "Besides, I'm not going to stay home, missing out on the adventure of a lifetime and let you have all the fun again."

"I just feel bad about putting you through this. We don't know what's going to happen, or how long we'll be. I don't even know we'll make it back alive."

"Last time you disappeared into space, I sat at home worried sick, not knowing where you were or if you were even alive. I'm not putting myself through that again. Besides, your best chance of getting out of this alive is with me. I'm a better shot then you are."

"True," I said. I looked into her bright green eyes, trying not to think of the horrors that may be awaiting us. "If anything happens to you, I..."

She put a finger on my mouth. "Shush. The feeling is mutual."

Just as I leaned over to kiss her, Monty shouted triumphantly from the front. "Found the cretins!"

I sighed as Donna grinned and pulled her head back. "Later," she said and started for the flight deck. We both joined Monty a moment later. He stabbed a finger at one of the round instruments in the dash. "There. I've got a lock on their trail. They're heading towards one of the moons of the ringed gas giant in your system."

"That would be Saturn," Donna said. "Sixth planet out from the sun."

"Correct," Monty said.

I stared at Donna in disbelief.

"Which moon?" Donna asked.

Monty tapped at one of the displays, and a ringed planet expanded into view, with a dozen smaller moons moving around it. "That one," he said, pointing.

Donna bent over to get a closer look. "That's Titan," she said.

"How do you know this stuff?" I asked.

She shrugged. "I've always been fascinated by astronomy. I used to have a telescope when I was a little girl."

"Strap in, kids," Montclair said. "We'll be accelerating shortly."

We got into seats and buckled up as Monty flipped switches and tapped numbers into a console. Then he pulled his goggles down over his eyes and, with a finger poised over a switch, asked, "Ready?"

"Monty, why do you need goggles inside a spaceship?" Donna asked.

"Tradition, my dear, and for effect." Then he flipped the switch and my back slammed into the chair. It felt like a twelve-hundred-pound gorilla was sitting on my chest.

We heard things crashing and banging in the corridor. "Oh dear, what's that?" Monty asked.

"We didn't get the supplies stowed away. They were still piled on the floor," Donna said.

"Blast. I forgot about that. We'll have a mess to clean up afterwards."

"How long does this last?" I asked.

"Oh, several hours. We have to catch up or we risk losing their trail."

A nasty thought occurred to me. "Won't they see us?"

"Don't worry, old chap. I won't get that close. I'll keep us inside the wake of their engines, the trail of particles we're following. They won't be able to detect us."

We lost the trail somewhere around Titan.

∞

It took us a few days to reach the vicinity of Saturn. Montclair didn't have to stay at the controls most of the time. Once the course was set, there wasn't much to do and he could leave the flight deck in the hands of the automated systems. The ship's systems would warn of any approaching objects.

We got the mess in the corridor cleaned up and the supplies safely stowed away. Some of the food was lost when the packaging broke and had to be jettisoned out an airlock. Someday, future explorers from Earth on their way to Saturn will be surprised to find SpaghettiOs and tomato sauce plastered against their windshield.

Montclair familiarized us with the ship, showing us the basics, such as preparing food in the galley and how the toilets worked. He even began to teach us how some of the ship's systems worked. Water, sewage, electrical, heat. We also learned some of the instruments on the flight deck so that we could help him. We had nothing but time on our hands and I wished I thought to pack a few paperback novels. His ship did have an extensive library in its memory banks, but it wasn't in English.

He started to teach Donna how to fly the ship. I tried to keep up with them, but quickly got bored. I spent my time familiarizing myself with Montclair's very interesting collection of personal weapons in his armaments room.

We sat in the flight deck as Montclair huddled over his screens. Donna sat next to him, peering into an instrument. Over the last two weeks, Monty had been tutoring her in the ship's instrumentation and operations. She had a real aptitude for it, and while she wasn't ready to fly solo yet, she proved an excellent student.

"How could you lose them?" I asked.

"The trail just vanished," Donna said, using an instrument to scan space around us. The thick white atmosphere of Titan came into view below, and behind it, the ringed planet of Saturn dominated the night, with its bands of multi-coloured clouds swirling through its atmosphere.

"Why would it vanish?"

"They may have shut down their engines," Montclair said. "But it would be unusual to do that, this close to such a powerful gravitational force like Saturn. Why would they pass this close to a gas giant? It would alter their course."

"Unless they wanted to use Saturn's gravity to change course," Donna said.

"No, with hyperdrives it's completely unnecessary. And a waste of time to come this way just to pass near Saturn on their way to another star system, unless.."

He fiddled with some knobs. "Unless there was something here they wanted. And the only object that can help them get to another star system is..." a few more twists of some knobs and a moment later he shouted: "Got it! There's a wormhole. I didn't see it at first until I adjusted my instruments to scan for one. But it's there all right."

I looked out the window. All I saw was Titan hanging in a star-filled black sky. "I don't see anything."

"It can't be seen with the unaided eye, but it's there. Right where the Rajnack trail ends. They've gone into that wormhole. That's where we must follow," he said.

"I wish I knew what you're talking about," I said.

"I've read about them," Donna said. "They're theoretically possible but the engineering is way beyond anything we have on Earth right now."

Montclair turned back to his console. "Yes, well, we'll have plenty of time for a lesson in relativity and space-time later. Right now we need to get through that wormhole. Buckle up!"

We buckled into our seats. Again, Donna got the front seat, and I was stuck in back. I was beginning to feel jealous and might have to call shotgun next time.

Montclair grabbed the joystick in front of him, moved it around a bit. I didn't feel it, but I could see we moved against the backdrop of Titan through the window.

"Hang on tight," he said. "This might get a bit rocky." And without waiting for an answer flipped a switch in the arm of his chair. The gorilla jumped back onto my chest as we shot forward. A few minutes later we vanished into the wormhole.

CHAPTER SEVEN

WE DIDN'T REALLY VANISH. But to an observer orbiting Titan it would have looked like it.

The vibrating shook us in our chairs like rag dolls and the entire ship shuddered as if it might come apart at the seams. I looked out the window. Titan was gone, along with all the stars.

"How long does this last?" Donna shouted, gripping the arms of her chair.

"It varies," Monty said. "Depends on how far the hole stretches through space-time. But it shouldn't be long. Even the biggest wormholes only take a few hours to transit."

An hour later the shaking stopped and the stars reappeared around us. Montclair immediately got busy with some instruments. "We need to determine our location and tr y to pick up the trail of our friends again. Donna, perhaps you could assist?"

Donna got busy, peering into the eyepiece of an instrument and turning knobs. I unstrapped from the chair and squeezed out. "I'll go back to cleaning guns," I said.

Neither of them responded as I left the flight deck.

Montclair had the most fascinating collection of personal weapons I'd ever seen. I still had my Ruger strapped into my shoulder harness, but I decided that getting to know Montclair's arsenal would be well worth the effort, considering what it was we were chasing across the galaxy.

He had several small handgun-sized weapons, long rifle-like energy weapons that required two hands, and a shoulder-mounted long tube similar to a bazooka. Not all of them were energy weapons. He also had some more traditional large-bore rifles that used exploding gases to fire a projectile, like guns back home.

The energy weapons didn't have rifled bores that required cleaning. I just made sure they were plugged in securely to their re-charging outlets. I wanted to be sure they were fully charged and ready when needed.

The lounge was one of my favorite places in the ship. It was a large sitting area off the main central corridor, lined with deep, thickly padded leather couches. There was more head room, it was open and spacious by Monty's standards, and had a nice view of the stars through several large windows. I came here often when the claustrophobia started to get to me, as most of his ship felt small and cramped.

But then, it was designed and built for Montclair sized people, not six-foot humans like myself.

I was sitting in the lounge, enjoying a nice cup of coffee while cleaning the rifle bore of a gun big enough to take out a tank when Donna's voice came over the intercom. "Jack, where are you?"

"In the lounge. Coffee's fresh, want some?"

"Can you come to the flight deck? We've run into a problem."

∞

"We've lost them," Monty said as I stepped into the control room. I stood behind his chair.

"How?" I asked.

"I was only able to pick up the slightest whiff of a particle trail, and then it completely dissipated. It's gone."

I looked out the windows at the vast empty space around us. Nothing but inky black and the tiny pinpricks of distant stars. No nearby star or planets. I felt as though Johnnie had disappeared for good into the depths of uncharted space.

"Which direction was the trail heading before you lost it?" I asked.

Montclair pointed out the window. "Straight ahead. I've oriented our ship in the direction they were heading."

One of the stars ahead appeared brighter than the others, but we were too far away to see any planets that might be in orbit around it. "Then we proceed in that direction, until we find a planet or asteroid or something that might be a destination point," I said.

"Or a wormhole," Monty said.

"And another thing," Donna said, looking up at me with worry in her eyes. "The advanced dissipation of the trail means the Rajnack are getting further ahead of us."

"It seems their ship is faster than I expected. They've made improvements in their engineering since my race last encountered them," Monty said.

"We're losing them?" I asked.

"Yes," Montclair said.

"Then we'd better hurry," I said, and buckled into the seat behind Donna.

Montclair drove the ship forward, following what was left of the particle trail. A few hours later the trail vanished completely. We continued on the same course, hoping upon hope we'd come to something.

The next day a star in front of us was noticeably brighter and had not shifted to either side. We were heading straight towards it on our present trajectory.

Two days later the star resolved into a large, orange yellow disk. Montclair brought the ship to a stop and Donna sat down in the co-pilot's seat next to him. "Help me scan the system for planets, Donna," Montclair said. "The Rajnack must have come here. There's nothing else around for parsecs."

They busied themselves with their instruments. I went into the galley to heat up some canned stew for dinner. Or lunch, or breakfast, or a midnight snack. I had no idea what meal it was or what time of day it might be. Of course, there was no 'day' out here. Any sense of a 24-hour rhythm was completely gone.

I made a meal and decided to call it lunch. Then I hailed them over the intercom. "Lunch is ready."

"Jack, where are you?" Donna asked.

"In the kitchen. Hungry?"

"We found something."

"I'll be right up." Leaving the trays inside the heating element that resembled a big microwave, I made my way forward.

"We found a planet, about ninety-two million miles from its sun," Donna said. "Thick atmosphere rich in oxygen, nitrogen, water moisture and other trace elements. Capable of supporting complex life."

"It's a good bet that's where they went," Montclair said.

"Our only bet. There's nothing else around," Donna added. "This has to be it."

Montclair set course, and we retired to the galley to eat the stew I'd so skillfully warmed up. After lunch I cleaned up, while the other two returned to their instruments on the flight deck. I went back to cleaning guns in the lounge.

Eighteen hours later we entered orbit over a greenish-brown desert world.

∞

I brought three steaming mugs with me to the flight deck. "Coffee anyone?" I said, starting to feel like the in-flight steward. The brown planet below filled the forward windows. Bits of white cloud drifted far below us, being chased by their shadows racing across a flat brown continent below.

But Donna and Montclair weren't looking out the window. They had their eyes on the instrument consoles.

"They have to be down there somewhere," Donna was saying.

I set a mug into the cup holders built into the arms of each of their flight seats. The continent below passed from flat desert-brown to green hills and darker green rivers.

"Any sign of intelligent life at all?" I asked. There was obviously water and plant life, which meant animal life was likely.

"No advanced infrastructure. A lot of villages and small, walled towns, with a simple network of dirt roads. A few larger cities, made of stone and wood, burning some kind of carbon for fuel, most likely wood or coal. I don't think these people have even discovered electricity yet. Not even combustion engines. This is a world that still lights and powers itself with fire. I'd set the level of this planet at early bronze-age."

"What would an advance race like the Rajnack want to trade with these people for?" I wondered aloud.

"That remains to be seen. But the silver lining around all this is that it should be very simple to locate them on the planet surface. The thermal signature of their engines will stand out against such a primitive backdrop. It will be the most powerful energy source on the surface. So in that sense we are lucky. Detecting their thermal signature against the backdrop of an advanced civilization, or even something like your Earth, Jack, would have been much more difficult."

I decided to let the veiled insult go by. "So what now?"

"We keep looking for the heat signature of their ship," Donna said.

It took another six hours before Donna found something. "Montclair, take a look at this," she said while looking at the sensors.

Monty got settled into the pilot's seat and peered into an eyepiece. "Where?"

"North end of that continent below us, on the west side at the base of the peninsula."

He adjusted a dial. "Yes."

"See the city on that large bay that looks like a foot?"

"Yes."

"There's a faint residue of isotopes, in the foothills just to the west of it. See it?"

He turned another dial. "Yes, got it. But it's too faint to be a ship."

"Not a ship," Donna said. "But the footprint of one. Those isotopes are the kind produced by a starship's drive. It could have been left by the Rajnack setting down there, and then lifting off again, like a footprint. It has to be. The local culture is way too primitive to have anything that could produce isotopes like that. They were down there, and then left."

"Yes, I see your point. Very good, we'd better check it out."

I stared out the window at the alien land mass below, hoping my son was down there, somewhere.

∞

Montclair wisely decided to land in the hills, instead of close to the village, so as not to alarm the locals by descending from the sky in a bright metal ship. But it meant we had some walking to do.

When we jumped out of the airlock of the cool, dry ship it felt like jumping into an oven, but after weeks inside Montclair's cramped ship, I didn't care. It was good to get out and look up at an open sky, even if it was a bit on the pinkish side with yellow clouds.

We stood outside the ship in the grass, overlooking a hot, dry savanna of tall grass and stunted trees. A herd of large four-legged herbivores moved lazily through the grassland below. They were about the size of elephants, with huge, humped backs and large heads low to the ground, faces in the grass. Their scaly dry skin was a dull brown and blended nicely with the surrounding landscape.

Montclair pointed down the slope to the bottom of the hill. "See that large flat area in the grass below, where it's been burned away."

Donna and I looked. He said: "The skin of their ship was still hot from re-entry and burned the grass when they landed. They came in too fast. There's also a residue of isotopes from their engines. That's where the Rajnack landed."

"So they were here briefly, and then left," I said. "I wonder why."

We stood for a minute looking around. Donna pointed across the grasslands. "See that village? There's smoke coming from it."

In the distance across the plains stood a village of tiny white domes surrounded by a wooden palisade. Nothing moved, but some of the buildings looked to be on fire.

"I think I know where the Rajnack went," Monty grunted. "A burning village this close to where they landed can't be a coincidence."

"Let's check it out. Maybe we can learn something," I said.

We started down the hill, wading through the tall grass. I had my Ruger. Montclair had two handguns inside his jacket, and Donna, very handy with rifles, had my Winchester. We also had universal translators clipped to our shoulders so we could communicate with the locals.

We reached the burnt spot at the bottom of the hill. The grass had been burnt away completely, exposing the dirt, which had been fused by intense heat. The whole area was ringed with blackened grass. There was nothing more to be learned that the ship's instruments had not told us, so we made for the village across the plain, passing through the herd of docile grass-eaters. On closer inspection they were hideous, reminding me of mammoth sized armadillos, covered in thick leathery skin. They had huge heads that narrowed down to snouts they used to forage through the grass.

"Careful of the wildlife. We don't know anything about the local animal life," Montclair said.

"It's the civilized variety of local life that has me worried," I said, as we walked towards the village ahead. We came upon a dirt path, joined by other paths as we drew nearer the village, and after a couple of hours we reached the village gate.

Or what was left of it. A wood palisade had surrounded the village, but most of it was burnt and knocked over. Only a few poles remained upright. The gate was burnt, and smoke still drifted up from its charred wood.

We picked our way carefully over the charred remains of the palisade. The village itself was a collection of small brightly painted domes of various sizes. They looked to be made of clay and varied in colour from white to yellow to bright red and deep blue.

The domes had small round windows and doors. Several of the ones nearby had their domes smashed in or lay completely in piles of rubble.

Several bodies littered the ground in front of us. They looked to be small furry mammals with long arms, wearing leather tunics and pants.

A deathly stillness hung heavy in the air, as if no one living remained, or those who lived hid in the shadows. We started walking down the empty street and followed its winding path through the town, passing by dome shaped buildings empty of life.

Eventually we came to an open square of wooden stalls that looked like a market. The stalls were filled with all manner of trade goods, from bolts of cloth and leather, clay pottery of all colours and shapes, to metal tools. Trinkets hanging on cords, stirred by the wind clanged from a stall, and in another stall a winged creature pecked at a rack of flesh hanging from a hook.

More small furry bodies littered the ground. "Where is everyone?" Donna asked aloud what we were all wondering.

We left the market and continued to follow what seemed to be the main street, and it wasn't long before we came to a section where the street narrowed. The buildings around us were domes built upon domes, like cascading multi-coloured bubbles, and the sun no longer reached us. It felt good to be out of the sun and get some relief from the heat.

A shadow moved inside a dark window nearby, and I stopped. Montclair and Donna, not seeing it, kept walking.

"Guys," I whispered. They stopped and turned. I nodded to the building next to me. "Something moved in there."

Montclair drew a pistol from his belt. "It may be one of the Rajnack. They've been known to leave their wounded behind."

"Or a villager," Donna said. "Either way, we might learn something."

Capturing one of the Rajnack crew would be an incredible win, I thought. We might find out where they were going. And maybe what they had in mind for Johnnie.

We moved towards the dome. It had a small round door of wood with a latch in the middle. "Donna, stay out here and watch the street," I said.

I got my Ruger out. Donna unslung the Winchester and took a position in the street. When she was ready, Monty grabbed the door latch and yanked it open. I jumped inside, holding the gun straight ahead. Monty followed me in.

It took us a moment for our eyes to adjust to the dim interior. There were small wooden tables and chairs, cabinets along one wall, and a small fire pit.

Something sat huddled against a wall, staring at us with large round eyes. My first impression was of a big koala bear, with a small black nose at the end of a short snout, and round ears atop its head. It had a thick torso covered in a leather tunic. Short pants covered its stout legs. Where it was not covered in leather, it had fine, light brown hair with yellow highlights.

In its paws it held a very large, curved blade.

We stood staring at it for a few minutes, and it stared back, blinking a few times.

Donna called to us from outside. "Guys, what's going on?"

"We found something. Or someone," I said.

Donna stuck her head in, looked around and then saw it. "Ahh, look at the cute teddy bear."

"It's a teddy bear with a big knife," Montclair pointed out.

"The poor thing must be terrified," she said and stepped inside. "Guys, put your guns away. You're scaring it."

We reluctantly holstered our handguns. The creature's mouth moved, and my earbud crackled. It said something but all I heard was garbled nonsense.

We left our translators on. A speaker attached to our shoulder allowed others to hear us in their language. Earbuds inside our ear translated the speaker's language into English for us, or in Montclair's case, his native language.

I tapped my ear. "Your translators aren't working."

"It must be an unknown language. That doesn't surprise me, as this is an uncharted planet. It will take a while for the software to learn the language."

"Great. How are we going to find out if these people know anything about the Rajnack?"

Donna took a few steps forward and crouched down to be at eye level. She held out a hand.

"Donna," I said. "Don't get too close. It might have rabies or something."

"Its frightened, that's all." Then, addressing the creature, she said: "Don't be afraid. We're not going to hurt you."

It didn't move or speak. Donna waited a minute, then sat cross legged on the floor, just out of arms reach. Then she took off her pack and brought out a cellophane package of cookies. She opened the package and got a cookie out. Then she held it out.

"We don't know anything about these creatures and what they eat," Montclair said.

"It's sugar and carbs. Pretty basic to any mammalian race, I'd think," Donna said.

The creature just looked back at her, then between me and Montclair. Donna ate the cookie and got out another one.

I could see this was going to take a while and no one was watching the street, which worried me. I didn't like the idea of getting caught by surprise, so I went outside.

I stood in the hot sun and looked up and down the empty street. The street was lined with discarded furniture, broken pottery, and overturned carts, like a lot of people had been trying to leave in a hurry at the same time. Nothing moved and even the air was still.

I found an overturned chair, set it up in the shade next to the wall, and got out a cigar. Montclair came out sometime later and found another chair. He sat next to me and got out his pipe. In a few minutes we were blowing smoke rings across the street.

"How's she making out in there?" I asked.

"Starting to make some progress, I think. The software is slowly picking up the language."

He looked around the empty street. "Where do you suppose everyone went?" Montclair asked.

"Maybe our new friend inside can tell us, but I'd bet almost anything the Rajnack had something to do with this."

About forty-five minutes later Donna opened the door and looked at us. "I need more cookies," she announced.

"How's it going?" I asked.

"Good, Orso has calmed down a lot. I think she's starting to trust me."

I handed her a package of cookies from my backpack. "Orso?"

"Yeah, that's her name, at least as near as I can pronounce it." She ducked back inside and shut the door.

We waited outside, smoking and blowing rings in the still air, not talking much at all. The shadows were growing long in the street, and I was starting to get hungry when Donna came back outside, followed by Orso.

"Well, at long last," Montclair said.

Orso bounced on its legs and chirped. I heard nothing in my earbuds but more garbled nonsense. "My translator still doesn't work," I said.

"She said she wants more cookies," Donna said.

"How come I couldn't understand it?"

"Her. Not it, but her. It might take a few minutes for your units to sync up with mine."

"What did you learn," I asked.

"It's what we thought. The sky monsters were here…" when she said 'sky monsters', Orso became noticeably agitated, jumping and twittering.

"Sky monsters?" I repeated.

"It's what they call the Rajnack. Monsters who terrorize them from the sky. It makes sense. They raided this town and took many of Orso's people. The ones that weren't captured by the sky monsters fled to the next town."

"The Rajnack are known for trading slaves," Montclair said.

"From what I learned from Orso, the Rajnack have been raiding this world since her great-grandmothers' day, coming to take people away. They are never seen again."

"Does Orso know where they went?" I asked.

"Yes, back into the sky."

"Then all we have to do is go back into space and pick up their trail," I said.

Montclair shook his head. "That won't work. Its been too long I'm afraid. The trail would have dissipated by now. Unfortunately, our quarry has got too big a lead on us."

"We could go back through the wormhole," Donna said.

"It may come to that, but it's a desperate move. We don't know that's where they went. And if they did, we don't know where they went from there," Montclair said.

"So we've lost the trail," Donna said, her voice tinged with sadness. "We have no idea where to go from here. What are we going to do?"

I stared down the narrow street, thinking. "We have options," I said. "We can go back to Earth and wait for them there. We'll have the time to come up with a rescue plan, but I hate to leave Johnnie with them that long."

"And there's another problem, Jack," Montclair said. "I hate to say this, but it must be figured into whatever we decide to do next. We have no guarantee they will return to Earth."

"I think they will. The coffee trade is too lucrative, and it wouldn't surprise me if they really do want to cut the Radauti out," I said.

"That may be right, but we have no guarantee Johnnie will still be with them when or if they return to Earth. They are out here to sell slaves. They might sell Johnnie at some point, along with the other slaves," Montclair said softly, as if afraid of giving voice to the horrible thought.

"I don't think they are out here on the fringes of civilization just to sell the coffee," I said. "No one out here can afford it. So I think at some point they will make their way back into the civilized regions of the galaxy to sell their cargo. We could head back there and see if we can pick up their trail."

"The galaxy is a big place, Jack, and the civilized worlds are far flung," Montclair said.

"Yes, but from what I've learned from the Radauti, there aren't that many worlds. And we could put the word out to the Radauti trade federation to keep an eye out. Someone is bound to notice Rajnack selling coffee. It's not at all usual."

"That could take a long time," Montclair pointed out, "considering the size of the galaxy. Johnnie may be a grown man before we find him."

"You checked the star maps when we arrived through the wormhole?" I asked.

Montclair nodded.

"Are there any other worlds nearby, which could be reached within a few weeks or months through normal space, without jumping through a wormhole?"

He shook his head. "The nearest other star system is years away, at best, even at near light speed."

I walked away down the street a bit, so I could think, and allow the tears I'd been fighting to flow freely. Head the wrong way and it might be years, if ever, before I find him. I stood at the end of the street, my back to the others, and made my decision. I was a detective – it was time to do some detecting.

Someone on this rock had to know something. After I dried my tears, I went back and told them what I wanted to do.

CHAPTER EIGHT

"THERE'S ANOTHER TOWN TO THE EAST OF HERE," I started to explain. "I saw it when we were coming down from orbit."

"Yes," Donna said. "The Rajnack have been coming here for a long time. Someone must know something about what they do or where they go with the captives they take. Let's go there, ask around, see what we can find out."

Montclair rubbed at his beard. "I don't know. It is, to use the common English vernacular, what you would call a 'long shot'."

"It's the only shot I can think of, other than going back home to wait there," I said.

"I think we should try," Donna said. "Our language synthesizers have picked up the language, so we can talk to the locals. We try that for a few days. If it doesn't work, then we head for home."

Montclair was quiet for a minute, staring off into the distance. Finally he grunted. "All right. I can't think of a better course of action. And your idea Jack would still get us back to Earth in plenty of time to plan a surprise for the Rajnack when they return."

With that settled we agreed to go back to the ship and wait for nightfall. Then, under cover of night, fly east and land someplace in the hills overlooking the town. We'd go into the town in the morning.

We retraced our steps following the street back the way we came. We passed through the smoldering wood of what remained of the palisade and entered the dry grasslands once again. The sun was still high but had progressed across the sky towards the eastern horizon.

When Orso realized we were leaving town and striking out across the grasslands she became agitated and refused to go any farther. Montclair and I went on a few more paces, but stopped and turned around when Donna didn't follow.

She'd stopped to talk to the creature. Orso was hopping up and down on her legs, chittering away.

"What's the matter?" I asked.

"She doesn't want to go out into the grassland. She says it's too late in the day for that now," Donna said.

"What does the time of day have to do with it?" I asked.

Donna left Orso and walked up to us. "She says its too dangerous at night. None of her people go out at night or start a long journey late in the day."

"Dangerous how?" Montclair said, looking around at the surrounding waste.

"The language synthesiser couldn't translate the words, so I didn't catch all of it. But she's very adamant that it's too dangerous. She wants to wait till morning."

"I really don't want to waste a night here. The days and nights are long, and I want to get to the next town as quick as we can."

"Sure, but Orso is trying to tell us we should wait for the morning. I think we should listen to her."

I looked around at the dry grassland. Giant sand dunes shimmered in the heat along the horizon. "We're armed to the teeth. You've got that rifle, I've got my Ruger and one of Montclair's energy powered handguns. And Montclair has a small armoury under his jacket. We've taken on Rajnack and lived to tell about it. I'm not afraid of some animal. I'd wager that any animal we meet out there will need to be more afraid of us."

"Okay, but I don't think these walls around the village are to keep others of her kind out, like a rival tribe," Donna said.

"If we hurry, we can get back to the ship before it gets too dark," Montclair said. "Let's be on our way."

Donna went back to talk to Orso. But when she rejoined us, Orso stayed in the shadows of the village. "She's terrified and won't come," Donna said. "So I said our goodbyes," she added, a little sadly.

I was disappointed also, although for more professional reasons. I'd have to manage with the locals in town tomorrow without Orso. Having her with me would have made it much easier.

We started down the road. We weren't very far when the road began to turn in the wrong direction, so we left it and struck out across the grassland, towards the brown hills where we'd left the ship.

Just then we heard loud chittering behind us. We turned around. We were still in sight of the road, and Orso came bouncing down it, left the road and came bounding through the grass towards us.

With her long arms she reminded me of a cross between a Koala Bear and an Orangutan. When she reached us she grabbed Donna's hand and chittered something. "She says she wants to stay with us and that we won't make it across without her," Donna said.

"That's big of her," I said.

"Don't be like that," Donna scolded. "She's worried for us."

"So, a teddy bear is going to protect us?"

Donna gave my shoulder a smack. "Stop that."

We resumed our trek across the savannah with Orso out in front. The sun beat down on us and sweat trickled down my back, soaking my shirt. I hadn't had a change of clothes since leaving Earth, and I was starting to feel pretty disgusting. I looked over at Donna as we walked through the waist high grass. She was as soaked as I was.

The herd of giant Armadillo-like creatures we spotted earlier were no longer in sight. The sun seemed to be moving too slowly across the sky, making the day feel surreally long.

And to add to the weirdness, it moved east, not west. Monty explained to me that this world turned slower on its axis, making its days much longer.

After a while we came across a small ravine with a dry riverbed at the bottom. It went in the general direction we wanted, so we decided to follow it. We scrambled down the slope. The sides were of loose, sandy soil, with grass roots exposed along the top. The bottom was rocky and firm, with little vegetation. We followed it for a while, and it continued to wind its way towards the hills we wanted to get to.

After a couple of hours of walking in the hot sun, we were all thirsty and soaked through with sweat. Our water canteens were dangerously low and Donna had been sharing what she had with Orso.

Our furry friend was panting and had unbuttoned her tunic. Montclair's hair, what I could see of it below his cap, was wet and stuck to the sides of his face and head. Donna looked as miserable as I felt.

My clothes clung to me, stuck to my skin with sweat. These were the only clothes I'd brought with me from Earth, and had been wearing them for weeks. Water on the ship was precious so there was little to spare for washing and I was starting to feel pretty disgusting.

After following the ravine for a while we heard what sounded like the trickling of water over rocks, and presently the ravine widened and opened into a wide meadow of lush, green grass. In the middle of the grassy meadow was a large pond of clear water, fed by a small trickle of water falling over rocks from above.

We stopped and drank in the vision for a moment. Donna didn't see the large creature drinking from the opposite shore across from us. She started to rush forward but I grabbed her arm.

"Careful," I said and nodded. "See."

She looked and her face went pale. Something with four legs stood at the shore with its head in the water. It had a long body low to the ground, supported on short, think legs and covered in scales.

"Don't anybody move," Montclair said as he slowly drew one of his weapons. "Only shoot if it gets hostile."

The creature seemed to take no notice of us and kept drinking. Donna got ready with her rifle, and I had my Ruger out. Then I noticed Orso was no longer with us.

"Where's Orso?" I asked.

Donna and Montclair looked around the ground. That's when we saw movement in the grass, making for the pond. The grass was too tall, or the critter too small, to see what was moving, but the grass shook and parted as something moved quickly towards the pond. Then Orso popped out from the grass and jumped into the water.

The large reptilian creature looked up at the splash, stared at us for a moment, then returned to its drinking. It clearly did not feel threatened by our presence.

That was either a good thing, or a very bad thing. I didn't yet have enough information to decide. It was huge, almost as large as an elephant. So maybe it decided we weren't big enough to be a threat. Or maybe it was a vicious predator that didn't feel threatened by anything.

Whatever it was, I hoped it was a vegan. I took comfort in the fact that Orso, who presumably would be familiar with the local wildlife, didn't think it was a danger. After she drank her fill she started doing summersaults in the water.

We holstered our weapons and walked up to the edge of the pond. The reptilian thing reminded me of a dinosaur, which I thought was pretty cool. I used Donna's cell phone to take a few pictures. I hoped I could show Johnnie sometime soon.

Montclair took his pack off and crouched down next to the water. "Don't anyone drink it until I make sure it's safe."

"Orso seems fine with it," I said.

Donna rolled her eyes. "You'd never survive long on an alien world without someone to watch over you. Orso is from this world. Just because its safe for her doesn't mean its safe for us. There are bound to be some differences in physiology."

"She's right, Jack. It will only take a moment to test it," Montclair said as he got something out of his pack. It looked like an instrument pack. He unscrewed the top and slid a glass tube out, filled it with water from the pond and slid it back into the instrument. He pushed some buttons and symbols appeared on a digital readout on its side.

He started reading out a list of chemicals, but it meant nothing to me. "Monty, in English please. Can we drink it or not?"

"It's perfectly safe," he said and stuck his face in the water. He splashed water over his head and neck, before drinking out of his cupped hands.

"Safe for us, as in us humans as well as you? I just want to avoid any misunderstanding," I said.

"Relax Jack. He said it was safe. Now, if you don't mind, I saw a secluded spot behind those bushes, and I'm going to get out of these clothes," Donna said.

The large reptile on the opposite bank slowly turned away and began to lumber up the sides, out of the ravine. Apparently, it was either a herbivore or wasn't hungry, and hadn't put us on its dinner menu.

"Donna, what are you doing?"

"Going to take a well-deserved bath."

"I wish you wouldn't. It's not a good idea."

She stopped and looked up at the sky without turning around. "And why don't you think it's a good idea?"

"Two reasons. We should stay within sight of each other. We don't know what dangers there may be around here. And second, we don't have the time. We're just stopping for a quick drink and to fill our canteens."

She turned on me, eyes flashing. "Jack Winters, I haven't been out of these clothes for weeks. I haven't washed, there's not enough water to spare on that stupid spaceship for washing clothes or bathing. I'm down to my last tampon and will have to start cutting strips of linen to make menstrual clothes. Women haven't had to do that since the dark ages. I've never felt so disgusting in my life."

I held up a hand. "I'm just saying, a bath would be nice but it's an unnecessary risk right now."

She took a step towards me, and I can't recall ever seeing her so livid. "Unnecessary? This may very well be our last chance before getting back into space. Once in space, I'll be stuck in these filthy clothes, with no chance of a bath. If I don't get a bath and wash my clothes, I'm going to kill something and right now you're my closest target. Your call."

I scratched the stubble on my chin. "Okay, well, since you put it that way, maybe a bath would be all right."

"Really? Gee thanks."

I smiled. "Look, in the interest of safety in numbers, maybe I should stay close and come with you," I said.

She didn't look in the least bit charmed. "Fat chance," she spat and turned away. I watched her walk along the shore and disappear behind some tall grass and bushes.

I went back and stood next to Montclair, who was sitting in the sand by the water. Orso was still splashing and somersaulting in the water nearby.

I got out my canteen and filled it up, then took a long drink. I started to feel like a bath might be a good idea. I left my backpack and guns on the shore and waded into the water. I went in until the water reached my waist, and then dunked down, completely submerging my head. It felt good.

I came back up. Montclair got out his pipe and struck a match. I watched him smoke, a very human habit. And then something occurred to me. We drank the same water, could eat the same food, breathe the same air. The entire time we'd been together, Montclair had not once had any trouble with our food. Not while we were on Earth. And his ship was now stocked mostly with canned food from Walmart.

"Montclair, what planet did you say you're from?"

He puffed out some blue smoke. "Actually, I never did specify."

"But you're an alien, right? I mean, from another planet."

"Correct, old chum." He puffed again.

I splashed more water over my face and head. "So what's your world like?"

"A bit cooler and damper than this one, I should say."

"What do you call it?"

"Loosely translated into your language, it means *Haven*."

"So how is it we can eat and drink everything the same, and breathe the same air? I mean, I'd expect some differences being that we're from different planets and all."

A cunning look came into his eyes as they narrowed. "You're very observant," he said. "But there's nothing to explain. Just a happy coincidence."

I thought for a moment before saying: "A pretty big coincidence. I'm not sure I buy it."

"Well, no matter old chap. It's worked out very well for our little joint venture. And it will stand you well when you come to my world to assist me in my quest."

"And all that 'old chap' stuff. You talk like some old English Earl or something. How's that?"

"It so happens that I learned English from a very old Englishman, although he wasn't an Earl. Some sort of Baron, I think."

"I didn't think they had Barons anymore."

"They still did in the sixteenth century," he said in a matter-of-fact tone.

I stared at him open mouthed, too stunned for a moment to ask the next question that would naturally occur to most normal people. But Donna's scream interrupted us before I could ask.

Chapter Nine

"Donna, what is it?" I yelled as I splashed back to shore. Montclair had already jumped from his rock and was running towards her.

"Just get here quick!" She said. I grabbed my gun, left the backpack, and ran as quickly as the uneven ground allowed. Orso was nowhere in sight.

I found Montclair standing at the edge of the water. Donna was still out in the water, up to her shoulders, pointing to the far side. "I saw something move in the water over there. It was big."

I looked but didn't see anything. "Maybe you should get out of the water."

"Not with you two standing there. I don't have anything on."

"I told you taking a bath was a bad idea."

"Go away so I can get out."

I shook my head and held my gun up. "I think I'd better stay here to protect you from any monsters that might be out there."

She started moving towards the shore. "Get behind those bushes and don't look," she said, just as a large gray hump broke the surface of the water, covered in scales.

It bobbed for a bit before going back under the surface. Donna was still turned towards us and she didn't see it. "Hurry!" I shouted, gesturing her to come in.

She turned to look. "Where?"

"I just saw it," I said.

Montclair aimed at the spot with his pistol but held his fire. "I strongly suggest you make all haste," he said, gun held ready. "And get to shore."

"Throw me my clothes," she said.

"Donna, this is no time for modesty," I said.

Water splashed out in the middle and a head appeared. The head was larger than a man's, about the size and shape of a horse, but scaly and with three round amphibian-like eyes. Long green vegetation hung from its mouth. It stared back at us, lazily chewing.

Montclair put his gun back. "I don't think it's dangerous," he said. "It's a herbivore."

I holstered my gun. "I wouldn't be so sure. I dated a vegetarian once. She turned out to be a real man-eater."

"I think I'll come out now, all the same," Donna said. She made a shooing motion with her hands. "Get away."

Montclair had been standing behind me a few feet. I turned around to go, but Montclair didn't move.

At first I thought he was getting cute with Donna, but that's not his style, and he wasn't looking down towards Donna in the water, but up at the far shore.

"Turn around very slowly, Jack. We have company," he whispered.

I turned around and looked across the small lake. A dozen or so creatures with spears were watching us from the top of the ravine on the far side.

At first, I thought they were extremely tall, then realized they were about human size, riding on the backs of other creatures which stood on two legs with bird-like heads atop long necks.

The riders were completely covered in dark greenish-brown cloth, like the surrounding terrain. Their faces were hidden by large hoods and all of them had long spears.

"Donna," I said quietly without moving. "Please get out of the water now."

She still faced us and hadn't seen the riders. She smirked. "Yeah, right. Now get out of here so I can get dressed."

"It would be best if we stayed right here," Montclair said. He hadn't taken his eyes off the far ridge, but his hand moved slowly inside his jacket. "Jack, get your weapon ready."

"You guys aren't being funny," Donna said and splashed water at us.

"Turn around, slowly, Donna and look across the lake," I said. The strange visitors hadn't moved.

"Has the big grass eating fish come closer?" She turned around. "I wonder what it looks like..."

She stopped in mid-sentence when she saw what stood on the other side. After a pause she finished the sentence with: "Oh crap."

"Get your clothes on," I said.

She started coming towards us, then stopped suddenly. "Jack."

"This is no time for modesty. Just get dressed so we can get out of here."

But she wasn't looking at me. "Jack," she said, and pointed up the hill behind us.

"They're behind us too, aren't they?"

She nodded. Montclair asked: "How many?"

"About another dozen."

I turned around. Montclair turned with me. The others were a lot closer, and we got a better look.

The hooded riders appeared to have long slim bodies under their robes. I could just make out the shapes of flat faces with dark eyes, peering at us from deep within their hoods. They held their spears down, pointed towards us.

The two-legged creatures they rode, on closer inspection, appeared to be reptilian, covered in green scaly skin with long tails and large, massive hind legs. They stood upright and had short front legs that ended in claws.

The heads were long and narrow with massive jaws, harnessed with leather straps. The riders sat in saddles strapped to the backs of their charges.

I heard Donna moving quickly behind me, pulling on her clothes. I said to Montclair: "This would be a really good time for that freezing trick of yours, like what you did at the police station."

"Unfortunately, I left the device in the ship."

"Why?"

"It doesn't work on Rajnack, so I assumed we'd have no need of it."

"Great. Get your pistol ready. If they attack, you take the six on the left, I'll take the rest on the right. Donna, get ready with your rifle and take care of the others behind us, on the far bank."

"Got it," I heard her say behind me.

I started reaching for the Ruger strapped to my shoulder when my arms were suddenly bound tight by a rope that snapped quickly around me. The force of the impact knocked me over, and as I went down I saw a spinning rope with balls at each end flying through the air. It hit Montclair in the chest, binding his arms, and he went down.

Hooded figures swarmed from the bushes beside us. I realized in a flash just how clever they'd been. While we had been distracted by the riders on the far bank, a dozen of them had used the cover of the bushes on either side of us to draw close and out-flank us, a classic military maneuver.

I looked at the cords binding me. Heavy round weights were tied to the ends. The aliens had used bolas. I twisted my head around towards Donna. She was on the ground as well, trussed as tight as I was.

The moment we were down, the riders on the ridge charged down the bank. I watched helplessly, unable to move enough to reach my handgun. One of them jumped out of his saddle and bent over me. He had a flat face of thick, leathery skin and narrow dark eyes and thin, narrow lips. He sniffed at me with a nose that wasn't much more than a small nub with holes. Then he quickly bound my legs and tied more ropes around my arms.

His hands quickly and efficiently searched my clothes and body. He found the Radauti timepiece on my wrist and removed it, and my heart sank. It went into the folds of his robes.

Next he took my knife. He found the handgun, looked it over curiously, and stuffed it inside his robes.

Knives and guns can be replaced, but the timepiece was irreplaceable. It had been my backup plan if things went wrong. Losing it was a crushing blow.

Gluplock had given it to me as a gift. The timepiece was many things, but most importantly it was my means of communicating with the Radauti. I could have used it to call them, but we had to leave Earth quickly to follow the Rajnack. And once we started following them, we didn't know where we'd be from one hour to the next, so we couldn't tell them where to meet.

And more than that, the timepiece *controlled* time – in certain limited ways. Limited time travel was possible, and the Radauti were learning how to use it. I had played around a little with it. It came in handy when unwanted guests arrived at the door, but it had its dangers and limitations, so it had to be used carefully.

And now it was gone, and I had no way to contact the only beings in the galaxy who could help us.

∞

Dozens of them carried us up the bank, trussed like pigs for the barbeque pit. A wagon with large wooden wheels and a cage waited for us in the tall grass at the top of the slope. One of them swung a door open and we were tossed inside.

My head hit the floorboards with a thud. I lay there for a few moments, slightly stunned, and waited for the sparkling in my eyes to subside. Behind me I heard the door shut with a loud clang and what sounded like the scratching of an iron key in a big lock.

I felt someone squirming against my back and I turned over. It was Donna, facing the other way. Montclair was on the other side of Donna.

"Donna," I whispered, not wanting our captors to hear me. She rolled over to face me, her eyes registering fear and pain. There were some scratches and slight bleeding on her arms.

"Are you all right?" I asked.

She attempted a smile. "I've had better days. You?"

"A little sore from the bolas," I said.

"I guess stopping for a bath wasn't such a good idea, eh?"

The wagon jolted and started moving over the rough ground. I called over to Montclair, but he didn't move.

"Can you reach Montclair?" I asked.

"I can't do anything with my hands and arms tied."

"Can you turn around and see if he's all right? He's not moving."

She rolled over and gave him a nudge with a knee. "Monty," she said. He didn't move.

She turned back to me. "There's no blood. He's not wounded that I can see."

"Hopefully he's just unconscious and will wake up soon."

The wagon moved slowly and we both struggled to a sitting position. It was too hard on our bodies to remain lying down, and our heads would have gotten banged and bruised from the bouncing.

Donna managed to sit next to Montclair, and used her bound hands to lift his head and slip a leg underneath to cushioned his head from the bouncing.

I wiggled over next to her, and we both sat with our backs to the side of the cage. "Have you seen Orso?" Donna asked.

"No, come to think of it, I haven't. I'm not sure where she's gone. I didn't notice her leave."

"What do you suppose they want?" She asked after a few minutes of silence.

"I don't know. But we're still alive, and that's something. If they wanted us dead, I think we'd be dead already. They went to a lot of trouble to capture us alive."

But I sounded more confident than I felt. The sky had turned a dark purple with the sun setting behind the hills, bringing this long day to a dreadful close, and I wondered if we would live long enough to see the sun rise again.

CHAPTER TEN

ORSO'S WORLD HAD NO MOONS. Night fell and we kept moving through the pitch black, surrounded by hooded figures with torches riding two-legged reptiles.

During the long afternoon I had kept track of the direction we moved, relative to the range of hills where we'd landed. But with nightfall I could no longer see the hills and lost all sense of direction. Even if we did manage to escape, I wouldn't know which way to run.

Sleep was impossible in the back of the wagon as it banged and jolted over the rough ground. Donna was little more than a shadow next to me, and we kept talking to keep our spirits up. Montclair finally roused and sat up with his back to the cage next to us.

At some point in the night we finally stopped and our captors made camp around us. They built a large fire and began roasting game. After they'd finished eating one of them came over and shoved a few scraps of meat through the bars towards us, but none of us had any appetite.

We watched as they unrolled blankets over the ground and settled in for the night. I wondered if they had guards posted somewhere out in the dark, or if they were now in 'friendly' territory and felt safe.

I waited until it looked like they were fast asleep. When none of them stirred for some time I whispered: "Can either of you move your wrists at all?"

"A bit," Donna said.

"I've been working on mine for some time now," Montclair said. "Not much luck, I'm afraid."

"Keep wriggling them as much as you can and see if you can work your way loose."

None of us were able to loosen the leather straps that bound us. We even tried sitting back-to-back, to use what little movement we had in our hands to work on each other's bindings, with no success. We eventually gave up out of sheer exhaustion.

Now that the wagon had stopped, sleep was possible. Montclair, propped up in the corner, shut his eyes and was soon snoring.

Donna rolled onto the floor and, using my leg as a pillow, drifted off to sleep. I sat with my back against the side of the cage, staring out into the black night, trying not to think of what might happen to us during the very short time we likely had left to live.

A shadow passed across some open ground between shrubs, close to the wagon.

I kept watching and the shadow emerged from a shrub and moved towards us. It reached the wagon and hopped up, grasping the bars across from me. It was small, about the size of a monkey, but not much more than a shadow. Then it disappeared below the wagon and was gone.

Curious local wildlife? I knew almost nothing about the animal life of this world and wondered, briefly, if I should be worried. But I soon decided that whatever it was, it couldn't be any worse than the creatures holding us prisoner. I leaned my head back against the bars and let myself doze off.

Movement at the back of the cage got my attention and I came fully awake. A minute later the door swung silently open and a small shadow jumped inside. It paused for a moment, then scurried across the floor towards us and stopped next to me.

I let my breath out in relief. "Orso," I said. Orso peered up at me with her large eyes, holding a big iron key in a paw. Then she bent over to sniff at Donna's hair and purred. She set the key down and pulled a knife out of her tunic and used it to cut the straps binding Donna's hands and arms. Then she cut the straps around her ankles.

Donna didn't stir and Orso nudged her gently. I moved my leg to give her head a shake and Donna came around. "Jack, what..."

She moved, as anyone naturally does when coming awake, and found that her arms and legs were free. "How..."

"Shhh," I said. "It's Orso."

Donna sat up and Orso wrapped her long arms around her and cooed. They hugged for a moment, then Donna used Orso's knife to cut me free. Then she shook Montclair awake and cut the leather straps from his arms and legs.

We all sat for a moment rubbing our wrists and ankles. "How did Orso manage to get the key?" I whispered. Donna said something to Orso, and then translated Orso's answer for us.

"I only know a few words of her language, but what I gather is that she hid in the grass when we were attacked and watched us get put into the cage. Then she followed us, and when the creature with the key fell asleep she crept up to him and cut it from his belt."

Monty grunted. "Very clever."

I looked around. "I think we'd better get out of here as quickly as possible, before one of them wakes up to take a pee or something."

Quietly we jumped down from the wagon. I shut the door so it wouldn't be immediately obvious we were gone, then we made for some nearby bushes and slipped away into the night.

None of us could see well in the dark, except Orso, who seemed to have good night vision and knew where she was going. We followed her through tall grass and brush, staying close so that we didn't get separated in the dark.

Every so often Orso, who could move much faster than the rest of us, would get too far ahead and have to circle back. She chittered at us, which came across as impatient scolding, but only Donna could understand her. Our captors had taken our translators along with everything else.

Which meant we had no water, and the sun would be up soon, baking us dry. We had no weapons, and I had no idea where we were in the dark. Soon it would be daylight and our disappearance would be discovered. They would be able to move much faster than we could on the backs of their reptilian ostriches.

Frankly, I didn't like the odds we'd make it through the day. It wouldn't be long before they ran us down and caught us again. And maybe this time they'd just kill us outright for the bother we'd caused them.

I kept these morbid thoughts to myself but I'm sure Donna and Montclair grasped our situation as well as I did.

Our one hope was Orso, a native of this area with excellent night vision. And she seemed to know exactly where she was going and chittered at us constantly. The ground under our feet started to rise and the tall grass gave way to rock and scrub brush.

We followed Orso up into the rocky hills, in single file. Donna was behind Orso, and I followed Donna. Montclair, the slowest of us, did his best to keep up. Hours passed, and Orso still urged us on. The ground got rockier and steeper and soon we were using both hands and feet to climb.

The sky to the west turned a faint pink, the light around us brightened a bit and we came to a flat section of ground behind some big rocks. We'd been moving non-stop for hours and needed a rest.

"Donna," I said. "Let's stop here for a minute."

She chittered something to Orso and sat down next to me against the rock. Orso scampered over and sat on Donna's lap as Montclair, puffing with labored breath, came around the rock and fell to the ground in front of us.

He wiped his forehead with the back of his hand. "Dear heavens, I don't think I've ever run so much in my life."

We hadn't, in fact, been running. Not a good idea in the dark over unfamiliar terrain. It was more like a fast walk, and we were only able to manage that thanks to Orso who led us safely through the dark. But for Monty's short legs, it probably had been running.

The sky was getting lighter and I stood up to have a look. The hill we'd climbed was a steep slope of rocky ground and scattered boulders, rising up from the brown desert valley below.

The bottom of the valley was still dusky, but I could make out the shapes of trees and the outline of a ravine, cutting its way across the valley floor below. There was no sign of pursuit, but I had to assume our abductors would be waking for the day and it wouldn't be long before our absence was discovered.

I wondered how important we were to them. How much effort would they put into chasing us? What did they want with us to begin with?

Donna chittered something as she stroked Orso's head. "Where'd you learn that?" I asked.

"I picked up a few words and phrases while using the translator."

I remained standing, leaning against the rock and watching the slope behind us. "What did you say?" I asked, without taking my eyes off the slope.

"I told her *thanks*."

"She seems to know where she's going," I said.

"Let's hope so," Donna said.

"I wonder how well our pursuers can track over rocky ground," Montclair said.

Small clouds of dust rose from the valley floor in the distance. "I think we're about to find out," I said.

Montclair climbed up onto the rock so he could see. "We'd better get moving," he said. Donna pointed up the hill and chittered something. Orso scampered up between some large rocks and we followed.

The rocky hill became a sheer cliff, too steep to climb, but Orso took us to a path that led into a narrow crevice in the rock wall. The path went up, steeply, between high rock walls, and this early in the day the sun had not risen high enough for light to penetrate the deep narrow crevice. We were plunged into cool dark shadow.

Eventually we emerged into a rocky hollow with broken stone and boulders scattered over its surface. There was no more hill above us. We'd reached the top and the end of our road.

"Now what?" Donna asked. Orso ran around the clearing in circles, going in no particular direction.

"I think the only way out of here is back down," I said. I went over to the side of the clearing and climbed over some rocks until I got to the edge and looked down. The sun had cleared the hills to the west and bright morning light reached the valley floor. The slope of our hill was long and steep, scattered with boulders and the occasional shrub clinging to life in the arid soil.

Several figures moved among the rocks below. They'd dismounted and were climbing up the hill towards us.

"Guys," I called and pointed.

The others joined me on the rock, including Orso. We watched them for a minute or so. "Well, Jack. Seems your question has been answered about how good they could track over rocky ground," Montclair said.

"We're trapped and we don't have any weapons," I said.

"We have lots of rocks," Donna said. "And they have to come up the same path we did."

We got busy gathering rocks, small enough to throw or push, and carried them to a ledge overlooking the narrow crevice through which the path passed. Donna went back to the side of the hill that overlooked the valley to be our lookout. Montclair and I stayed by the cliff's edge with our rocks, ready to throw them down onto the heads of our pursuers.

"What do you think our chances are?" I asked Montclair as we waited.

Montclair stroked his beard. "I think we're doing the best we can."

"Yeah, that's about what I thought too."

"Even in the face of apparent futility and hopelessness, one must never give up. Have faith, Jack Winters."

"It's been good knowing you, Montclair. I'm sorry it came to this."

Donna ran up to us. "Any minute now," she whispered.

We each got ready with a rock and crouched at the edge of the cliff. Something scratched against the rocks below, followed by dark brown robes climbing up the path. More followed, until the crevice below swarmed with them.

"Now!" I shouted and pushed a boulder over the edge. It was heavy and I needed to stand and use both hands to get it over the side. It bounced against the sides of the crevice and dropped onto the path below, striking one of our pursuers. He crumpled to the ground howling in rage and pain.

We rained rocks down on their heads. The crevice was narrow – barely wide enough for a man, or in this case humanoid – so it was impossible to miss hitting someone below. The perfect place for an ambush.

We threw rocks as fast as we could, but there were too many of them and only three of us. Orso had disappeared again, not that I expected her to fight with us.

It was ultimately futile, of course, as we knew it would be. But what else could we do?

Several attackers fell to the ground, struck by rocks, but more jumped over their prone bodies and surged forward. The battle had only lasted a few minutes and already several were in the hollow behind us. Spears started striking the rocks around us and we were forced to pull back from the ledge overlooking the crevice.

One of the humanoids charged up the slope from the hollow, spear thrust forward, dark robes rippling in the wind behind him. His hood had fallen back, revealing a face that could inspire a series of horror films. Ghostly white, with deep sunken dark eyes and forward jutting jaws. Its teeth were long and sharp over its lower lip.

I saw it first and yelled for the others to run. Montclair, for all his stockiness, proved quite nimble. He grabbed a spear from the ground and ran towards the creature rushing up the hill towards us.

A bolo came spinning through the air towards me, forcing me to jump aside as another creature ran up the hill with spear in hand. I grabbed a rock in each hand and waited. I lost sight of Donna.

The thing reached me and thrust its spear forward, forcing me to jump back. His lips widened in a malevolent grimace as he stepped closer. I heaved one of my rocks at it, which he dodged easily but in so doing was momentarily off balance.

In that instant I charged, got around the end of the spear while he was still off balance, and smashed the side of its head with the other rock in my left hand.

He screamed, stumbled back and let the spear drop. I reached down, grabbed the spear and thrust him through. I pulled the spear out of his chest and he collapsed to the ground.

I looked around for Donna and spotted her about thirty feet away. She'd fallen and was on her hands and knees, trying to get back up. More creatures swarmed up the slope towards us and I started running towards Donna, but one of the creatures got to her first.

It shrieked with delight, the primal howl of a predator taking joy in its kill, and put a foot on her back. He pushed her down and held her flat against the ground. It raised its spear and got ready to plunge it down into Donna's back.

I kept running, holding the spear forward in both my hands, but I was too far. I'd never reach her in time, but still I ran, watching the humanoid lift the spear a bit higher.

At that moment a bundle of fur and legs flew across the air from the top of a nearby boulder, screaming with rage towards the attacker. The creature, surprised and thrown off balance, dropped his spear and stumbled backwards with Orso's arms wrapped around its face.

They fell over together as I reached Donna, just as several more attackers came up the slope. I helped her up. "Are you all right?"

She looked around at the slope below us, swarming with nasty humanoids. "Oh, yeah. Never better." She bent over, grabbed a rock in each hand, and then stood next to me. I stood with the spear pointed forward, waiting.

The humanoid rolled down the slope with Orso still clinging tightly to his head. Another humanoid stepped up and thrust his spear into Orso's back. Orso screamed and went limp, releasing her grip, and the creature used the end of his spear to pick Orso up and hold her high, before flinging her away like a rag doll.

"Orso!" Donna yelled. She started to run forward but I grabbed her arm and held her back.

"There's too many," I said, looking at the swarm of ghastly creatures coming up the hill. They paused long enough to form a rough skirmish line and then started to advance towards us.

Montclair appeared at my side, holding a spear. "Where have you been?" I asked.

"Busy liberating this spear from its former owner," he said, and added grimly: "He won't be needing it any longer."

The three of us stood side by side, watching the skirmish line of a dozen attackers approach slowly up the hill. There was no place to run. "Well, honey, this isn't exactly how I thought things would end for us," I said. "I was hoping we'd end up dying of boredom as PTA committee volunteers."

"It certainly hasn't been boring, has it dear?"

Our attackers stopped several paces away and grinned at us. Several began to howl and shake their spears. It seemed to me they were delaying the final kill, as if to relish the moment, the way a man might slow down with the last few bites of a good steak, not wanting it to end.

Just then a series of loud pops erupted from some bushes to our left, and several of the attackers fell to the ground, decimating their skirmish line.

Those left standing looked around, startled. This time they howled not with delight, but in fear. A short stout figure stepped out from the bushes, holding a gun, flame erupting from its muzzle, and the rest of the skirmish line went down. The two or three remaining turned and fled down the hill and disappeared into the crevice.

Our rescuer turned to us and pulled back his hood to reveal a face covered in short fur, with large eyes on either side of a protruding face. He had long whiskers that hung down from the end of his jaw and short floppy ears sticking up from his head.

His body was stout, and he stood about the same height as Montclair, not including the ears. He wore a brown leather tunic and loose-fitting baggy black pants. He looked like a caricature from a fantasy novel, but the machine gun in his hands was real enough.

For all his strangeness I knew what he was. I'd met his kind before on the mining colony of Carimeth.

"My name is Gurth, and I see I came just in time," he said in perfect English.

CHAPTER ELEVEN

DONNA IGNORED GURTH and rushed down the hill to Orso. She dropped to her knees at Orso's side, picked her up and cradled her in her arms. I went over and stood next to her, placing my hand on her shoulder.

Orso was completely limp in Donna's arms. She looked up at me with wet eyes. "She's dead Jack."

I gave her shoulder a squeeze. "I'm sorry," I said.

"She saved my life."

Montclair joined us and stood on Donna's other side. "She turned out to be a true friend."

None of us knew what else to say, so we stood with Donna in silence. The stranger joined us after a few minutes. "We mustn't stay," he said. "The Desert People may return in greater numbers."

I looked down at Donna and squeezed her shoulder gently. "He's right. We'd better get going."

"We can't just leave her body to rot amongst these evil creatures. She deserves better than that," Donna said.

"There is a cave nearby," Gurth said. "We'll take her there."

∞

Gurth led us to a cave where we laid Orso down and gathered around her body. After a few minutes of silence I looked at Gurth. His species, the Whoolnor, was not native to this world but he looked like he'd been here for a long time.

"Do you know Orso's people?" I asked him.

Gurth grunted. "I've lived nearby for more years than I care to remember."

"We just arrived and know nothing of their ways. I was hoping you might know something of their burial customs," I said.

"Yes, indeed. They are quite elaborate. Because of the hot climate, they burn the deceased quickly, within a few hours of death, on a funeral pyre out in the desert. This is followed by a celebration in town that can last several days, in which the life story, adventures and accomplishments of the departed is re-enacted in stage plays."

Montclair and I traded looks, and we were both thinking the same thing. "That's not practical for us, and a fire that size will be visible for miles. More Desert People will see it. The risk is too great."

"We have to do something," Donna said. "We can't just leave her like this on the ground."

"We can't dig a grave, not without tools in this hard ground," I said. "Even with shovels it will take too long."

Gurth gestured with his hands around us. "There are plenty of loose rocks."

So we gathered up rocks and placed them over Orso, until she was completely covered under a large mound. When the chore was complete we stood in front of the rock pile.

"I don't know what kind of religion or sacred text Orso may have had, but I'd like to quote Jesus Christ," Donna said. "I think it stands true for all peoples and species. 'Greater love has no one than this, that one should lay down their life for their friends.'"

Montclair and I followed with a few words, and then it was time to leave Orso to her eternal rest.

∞

We gathered just outside the mouth of the cave. After the cool interior, the heat outside felt even more oppressive. "We haven't had a chance to properly thank you," I said to Gurth. "We'd all be dead if you hadn't come along when you did."

"That's true, yes. You did manage to get yourselves in quite the bind," Gurth said without a trace of humour.

"Ah...well, thanks," I said.

"Yes, thank you very much," Donna said. Then: "Are you from around here?"

"I'm not from this planet, if that's what you mean," Gurth said. "But I have been living in these hills for many years now."

"Where do you come from?" She asked eagerly. Donna was nothing if not curious.

"There will be time for all your questions later. I have several myself, but not here! We must be going," Gurth said.

Montclair bowed. "You have my deepest appreciation. If there is anything I can do for you, I'd be honoured to do what I can."

Gurth rubbed the whiskers on his chin. "Well, about that. There is something you can do for me, but this isn't the place to talk. Let's get out of the heat and away from the Desert People."

"We need to be getting back to our ship," I said, looking around at the hills in the sudden realization I had no idea which direction it lay.

"Yes, of course. But your ship is a day's journey. You'll never make it in this heat without food and water. And the Desert People are between you and your ship."

"We have no choice but to try," Montclair said, straightening his back.

"I wouldn't advise it. You'll likely end up as carrion for airborne scavengers," Gurth said. "Or worse, prisoners of the Desert People."

"Maybe, but we have to try. We came to this world tracking a Rajnack ship. They have my son. We need to get back to our ship quickly," I said.

A cunning look entered his eyes. "Yes, I know all about the Rajnack. And I think I know where they've taken your son."

I practically jumped out of my skin. "You do? How could you know that? Where did they take him?"

"We can't talk here. Come back to my bothi for the night. It's on the way to your ship and I'll take you there in the morning."

"How could you possibly know where they've taken my son?" I repeated.

"We're in no mood for word puzzles," Montclair said gruffly, with a guarded look. "Speak plainly or we'll be on our way, with or without you."

Gurth's ears twitched. "The Rajnack operate a mining colony on a planet not too far from here, astronomically speaking. Considering its close proximity, I'm certain the Rajnack ship you pursue will make that their next stop. The only other Rajnack world is several months away, so they won't miss the opportunity. We can probably catch them there, but we must be quick. We must reach my bothi before dark! Come quickly now!"

And with that he started down the side of the hill, moving quickly around the rocks and boulders that littered the landscape.

Donna, Monty and I just looked at each other for a moment. Donna raised an eyebrow. Monty shrugged a shoulder. "Well, what choice do we have? I don't see that we have any better options," he said.

We nodded in agreement and followed the strange Gurth down the hill.

For the first little while Donna peppered him with questions. Where was he from? How did he come to this world? How did he find us? Who were the Desert People and what did they want with us? How did he know English?

And surely he must have been curious about us, with many of his own questions. He knew we weren't from this world. Didn't he want to know where we were from and why we were here? But he seemed content to walk in silence, ignoring all her questions, saying only that 'there will be time for talk later.'

We walked all afternoon, making our way up and down slopes of loose rock and dry, parched soil. I thought the hills would never end, and the sun seemed to make little progress across the sky as it beat down upon us. At one point we stopped at a small spring of water, at the bottom of a gully deep between two hillsides. A few shrubs and tall grasses clung to life in the soil around it. We stopped to drink and Gurth refilled his water pouch.

After a short rest we resumed our march. Montclair came up beside me. Gurth and Donna walked ahead a little. "He's not very talkative, is he?" he whispered.

I didn't say anything.

"I'm just saying, he's very closed with his information, if you get my meaning," he added.

"You're being overly cynical," I said.

"Well, I'll say no more of the matter."

I looked at him. "That would be lovely," I said as we began climbing yet another barren slope. *Would these hills ever come to an end?*

∞

Eventually we came to a wide cleft in the rock, hidden deep in the hills. And in the cleft, under an overhang of thick rock, sat a cluster of four domes made of white clay.

Gurth stopped and turned to us. "Welcome to my bothi," he said. "Please feel at home." He looked up at the sky, where the sun was finally approaching the horizon. "We'll rest here tonight and make for your ship in the morning."

Then he opened the round wooden door in the nearest hut and went inside, leaving it open in an invitation for us to follow.

Donna went inside. Montclair and I remained outside for a minute, taking in the surroundings. "He seems very intent on my ship," Montclair said. "I don't like it."

I had several reservations myself, wondering why this complete stranger would go to so much trouble and risk to rescue us from the Desert People, then bring us here. If he'd been Radauti, I wouldn't have had any reservations. The Radauti are highly principled and altruistic people. But I'd met Gurth's kind on Carimeth, and I knew well enough that they did not possess the altruism of the Radauti, or even the measure that better humans are capable of.

I privately suspected Gurth had not done all this out of the kindness of his heart and there'd be a price he'd seek to extract from us. But I didn't say any of this to Montclair. He was already paranoid enough, so I followed Donna inside without saying anything, leaving him outside to fret on his own.

The cool dark interior was a relief from the blistering sun outside. Small slits high in the walls let in some light, showing a Spartan interior. Rugs of fur from unknown animals covered the floor, arranged around a low wooden table. There was a small fireplace, pegs from which clothes hung, and shelves with clay jars.

Our host busied himself setting the table, bringing out plates of dark, dried meat from a cupboard. He went outside and returned a few minutes later with jars of water. He set the jars down on the table and got cups from a shelf. From another shelf he retrieved a few more jars. Soon the table was set with a simple feast of dried meat, nuts, dried fruit and water.

He sat down on a rug in front of the table and gestured. "Please," he said. "Help yourselves. You must be hungry and thirsty."

Donna sat down and picked up a slice of meat from the platter and took a tentative bite. She chewed, and then started eating faster. I sat down next to her and picked up a piece of meat. It was thin and hard, like jerky back home. I often made jerky myself after a successful hunting trip.

Montclair came in, and the four of us ate and drank with little conversation. But the questions gnawed at me, and the Rajnack who had Johnnie were still out there somewhere, getting further away by the moment. I wasn't in the mood for any more delays.

"You said you knew where the Rajnack had taken my son," I said.

Gurth took a nut out of a bowl and tossed it into his mouth. He chewed thoughtfully. "Yes, that is true."

"How do you know this?"

"Because I know where they take all their prisoners, and it's not far from here."

"Are you certain?" Montclair asked.

"Yes," he said simply. "I have little doubt."

Gurth went on to explain. "The Rajnack have a colony world not far from here, rich in minerals and heavy metals. The work is very dangerous, and they use a lot of slave labor. They come here on raids to collect slaves from among Orso's people. They are small, but very strong, making them ideal for the underground tunnels, and they have excellent night vision, useful in the darkness underground."

"The Rajnack come to this world on a regular basis to take slaves. If the Rajnack party you are tracking stopped here, then their next stop will almost certainly be this colony world. It's the only other world nearby, and they can refuel and resupply there. They won't miss stopping at that port."

"How do you know all this?" Donna asked, fascination in her voice.

"Because I was once a prisoner on that world, forced to work as a slave."

"But you are here now," Montclair pointed out, if not a bit suspiciously.

Gurth twitched a whisker. "Correct. How observant of you!"

Montclair's face turned red. "I just meant, how did you come to be here?"

"I escaped years ago, in a small scout ship I'd stolen, and fled here. There wasn't much fuel in the ship and it was damaged in the escape. This was as far as I could make it. I was lucky to get this far, and the ship was damaged beyond repair when I crashed in the desert. That was twenty years ago, as this world circles its sun. I've been stranded here ever since, with no way to communicate with the outside galaxy or call for help. Until you came along, Rajnack raiding parties were the only ones who ever visited this miserable little planet. I don't think anyone else knows of it."

"How did you find us?" I asked.

"Find you!" Gurth barked. "The whole country saw your shiny bronze ship gleaming in the bright afternoon sun as you descended from the sky. I stood outside and watched you land in the hills not far from here. The Desert People would have seen you coming too, and would have known you weren't Rajnack. No doubt they'd been hunting for you when they caught you. It wasn't an accident that they came upon you. You are lucky the Rajnack had already left, or they would have seen you too, and likely as not shot you out of the sky. The next time you come to an unknown planet hunting a dangerous predator like the Rajnack, I'd advise you to be more discrete."

"Who are the Desert People? What did they want with us?" Donna asked.

"Desert People are the worst scum and villains on this miserable world. Slave traders, thieves and murderers. They trade with the Rajnack, trading slaves for trinkets. They will capture Orso's people and hold them for the Rajnack. They wanted you for trade with the Rajnack. That's the only reason they didn't just kill you outright when they found you. You were more valuable to them alive than dead."

"How did you become enslaved?" I asked.

"A long time ago, when I was a lad, I was travelling with my parents and relatives to a new world. But a Rajnack raider caught us and captured everyone on board that wasn't killed in the firefight. My parents were killed defending me. Only a few of my relatives survived and they all later died as slaves on the prison world. I am the only one of my brood to survive."

We were all stunned at the tragic story. After eating in silence for a few minutes I asked: "You will know something of how I feel, then, with the kidnapping of my son. Tell us how to find this world so that I can go get him."

"I'll do better than that. I'll go with you and guide you there myself."

Montclair said: "That's very generous of you, but it's not necessary for you to come. Our ship is small and we don't have room for extra passengers. I have star charts on the ship, though, and we can use those. You can show us on the star charts."

He shook his head. "It's uncharted. You won't find it on any of your maps." Then he leaned forward and placed his paws on the table, partially lifting himself from the floor. "I've rotted in isolation on this remote planet long enough. Do you really expect me to remain content to stay behind?"

"No, of course not," I said quickly. "We won't abandon you. We'll come back for you, or send help once we've got Johnnie."

"That's not good enough. I must have revenge on the Rajnack and restore my honour."

"Killing Rajnack won't bring your family back," I said. "But my son is still alive and that's my first priority."

A fire kindled in his eyes. "You don't seem to understand. I'm not asking. The only way I will tell you where the Rajnack have gone is if you take me there. If you won't take me, I won't tell you anything."

"Assuming we take you, what do you have in mind?" Monty asked.

"Help rescue your son and kill many Rajnack along the way," Gurth growled.

I exchanged looks with Donna and Montclair. "Montclair, what do you say? It's your ship."

He stroked his chin and thought. Then his bright eyes fixed on mine. "Jack Winters, I made a solemn oath to help you get your son, and that's what I will do."

I looked at Gurth. "Then we are agreed. We have a deal."

"Our little quest has just gained another member," Montclair said, and took a bite of jerky.

Gurth nodded in satisfaction. "We'll leave at first light. Your ship is not far, and we should be there before midday."

"And how far is this planet you're taking us?" Montclair asked.

"Do you have a light-drive?"

"Yes, of course. Radauti engineered."

"Then it won't take long. We need just one more item." With that he grabbed his coat from a peg by the door, and a bag from the floor. He opened the door and turned to us.

It was pitch dark outside and the stars of strange constellations shone in the night sky behind Gurth through the open door. "I will be back in an hour or so. Make yourselves at home." With that, he turned around and disappeared into the night.

"Now where do you suppose he's gone off to?" Montclair said, staring at the open door. Donna got up and closed it. "I'm not sure we can trust him," she said. "He seems hell bent on vengeance. It makes me wonder what he really has in mind."

"Cut him some slack. He spent years as their slave after they murdered his family. And for the last twenty years he's been stranded on the backside of a desert on an isolated world, where the only visitors are Rajnack raiders. I'd be a bit twitchy too."

Montclair said: "Well, for better or worse, we're stuck with him."

∞

About an hour later the door banged open and Gurth walked in. Donna, Monty and I had taken a pile of furs from the corner and laid them on the floor in front of the fire. It wasn't cold, but the thick layers of fur made for a very comfortable mattress to lie on, and we were asleep in seconds.

I sat up with a start at the sound of the door. Monty groaned and sat up as well. Donna mumbled something in a half-sleep and rolled over.

Gurth took something from his bag and set it on the table. "Do you think you can hook this up to the power grid on your ship?"

Monty and I got to our feet and went over. It was a black metal device about a foot long. Wires stuck out of it. I had no clue, but Monty looked like he knew. "A transponder," he said.

"Yes, from the Rajnack ship I came here in. I think it will still work."

Monty picked it up and turned it around in his hands. "I'll have to modify the power coupling, but yes, I could probably get this powered up."

They both looked at each other significantly, like it meant something important. "I don't get it. What is this?" I asked.

"It transmits a signal that their radar and defense systems will recognize as one of their own. It means we will look like a Rajnack ship on radar. This will allow us to approach their planet safely, without making them suspicious," Monty said.

"But your ship looks nothing like one of theirs," I said.

"That only matters if we get too close, which in space is very rare. We'll just keep our distance."

"Their colony is in a nearby system," Gurth said. "We should be there before the sun of this world has dipped below the horizon ten times."

"Okay, well, the days here are six hours longer than Earths, so call it three hundred hours or so," I said, doing the math out loud.

"I've been waiting all these years for a chance to avenge myself and my family," he said through clenched teeth. "And now I will have it."

I stared at our host for a moment, taken aback with the heat of his vehemence, and asked myself what we'd gotten ourselves into.

As it turned out, my math wasn't far off. It took us three hundred and eleven hours to reach the Rajnack slave world.

CHAPTER TWELVE

MONTCLAIR SAT IN HIS PILOT'S CHAIR and leaned over an instrument. "There are several space craft down there," he said, adjusting a brass knob between his thumb and index finger.

The four of us crammed onto the flight deck to have a look at the Rajnack colony below. Donna had the co-pilot's seat. Gurth and I had the jumper seats behind them and looked out the windows while Donna and Monty used the instruments.

An empty, dark world, passed below. Thick grey clouds swirled over vast tracts of barren rock and the occasional dark lake.

Presently a green patch came into view, partially obscured by clouds. We could see roads, buildings and a large dark rectangular strip with white lines. Small shiny objects glinted in the sunlight on the dark strip.

"I'm scanning the area around the spaceport," Donna said. "There are clusters of small buildings close by, surrounded by large buildings with huge heat signatures."

"The large buildings are the agricultural collectives," Gurth said. "The smaller ones are residences and administrative offices."

"Ah! I think I see it," Monty said. He made a few more adjustments, then leaned back in his seat with a satisfied grin. "Our friends are down there, all right."

"Are you sure?" I asked.

He nodded. "Thermal signatures of ships are unique, like fingerprints. Its the Rajnack ship we've been chasing. I'm sure of it."

"Now to find Johnnie. He could be anywhere down there," I said.

Gurth rubbed at his whiskers. "Most of the population is concentrated in and around the spaceport. I would begin there, starting with the spaceship itself. There is a good chance Johnnie is still on board, since he wasn't brought here to be used as a slave. He is their leverage over you. So, they probably intend to keep him. I think that ship is our best place to start looking."

"We don't exactly blend very well with the locals," Donna said. "How will we move around down there?"

"There is a large population of slaves brought from my world, and other worlds including Earth. They will be used to seeing humans, and many of them speak your language," Gurth said.

"That explains how you know English," Donna said.

"Yes. I learned it from human slaves," he said.

I'd become so accustomed to Gurth speaking English that it'd slipped my mind how odd it was to arrive on a distant planet and find an alien speaking perfectly good English. But then the Radauti were also very fluent in my language, so I'd gotten used to it.

"We need a plan," Donna said. "We can't just go charging down there."

"I've been thinking about that," I said. "But we need a way down to the surface undetected."

Monty nodded and rubbed his chin. "There's a way. We can use the escape pod."

"Good. Then once I'm down I'll make my way to the spaceport and get eyes on our Rajnack ship. I'll disguise myself as a slave and blend in with the humans. Maybe I can get inside the ship pretending to be a slave bringing something on board. Hard to say, I won't really know until I get down there and have a look."

"That could work," Monty said.

"Meanwhile, you guys stay in orbit," I said. "Once I find Johnnie, we'll get someplace away from the spaceport and signal you. You come down, pick us up, and we head for Earth lickety-split. We'll be gone before the Rajnack even knew we were here."

"Head for Earth!" Gurth said. "Why run? Once we have your child, we can blast the colony to dust."

I shook my head. "We have to assume the Rajnack will give chase, so we don't want to stick around. And blasting the town will kill a lot of innocent people."

"My ship does not have blasters," Montclair added. "It has a few defensive systems, but this isn't a battleship. It doesn't have heavy weapons capable of attacking planets. Not that I would use them even if it did."

"We don't need blasters and laser canons. This area of space is littered with asteroids," Gurth said. "All we have to do is grab one, bring it back and drop it on them. A large enough rock will make a kinetic weapon equal to several atomic bombs. It is easily done. It would obliterate the entire colony and turn their spaceport into molten rock."

"Are you crazy? That's genocide," Donna shouted. "It would kill everyone below, including all the slaves. We would be massacring thousands."

"Not to mention the wrath it would bring upon us from the Rajnack," Montclair said. "It is sure to spark a war. If we start dropping asteroids on them from space, what is to stop them from returning the favor? Millions could die in the ensuing wars."

I thought about the lengths the Rajnack went to avenge the death of just one of their sisters. I shuddered to think what they might do if we killed off an entire colony world. Montclair was right.

But Gurth's eyes were dark and cold. "It's a risk worth taking. War with those monsters is inevitable anyway. We may as well start it now. We have reason enough. Look at the thousands of slaves they've taken," he shouted. "The Rajnack deserve to die after what they've done."

"You're insane," Donna said.

"I don't think we should be so quick to pass judgement on who deserves to die," Monty said.

Gurth looked at me. "Don't you want your son back? Don't you want to avenge him?"

"Yes, I want him back. But not at the cost of thousands or millions of lives."

"It's a small price to pay for honour," he said.

"I won't have any part of your twisted idea of honour and lust for revenge," Montclair growled.

Gurth clenched his fists and growled: "I brought you here in good faith so that you could help me."

"Yes, but you said nothing about destroying the entire colony and sparking inter-galactic war!" Montclair spat back.

Gurth got out of his seat and stormed off the flight deck. We watched him go. "I knew bringing him was a mistake," Montclair said, looking at the door Gurth had slammed shut behind him.

"We had no choice," I said. "We needed him to find this colony. Let him go, he'll cool off in a while. Now, about my plan. What do you think?"

Donna said: "Good plan, except one thing. I'm coming with you. Monty and Gurth can stay up here."

I shook my head. "I'm going down alone."

But I could see she wasn't about to be easily put off. She remained sitting in the co-pilots chair, crossed her arms and glared at me. "With two people on the surface we can double the chances of finding Johnnie."

I leaned over and took her hand. "I don't know what I'm going to find once I'm down there. I'll have enough to think about without worrying about you. I'll work much better alone, knowing you're safe. Besides, you're getting pretty handy with the ship. You'll be more useful up here."

She pushed my hand away and stood up. "Don't patronize me. How do you think I feel about you going alone, with no one to cover your back? What if you get hurt?"

Tears welled around her eyes. Donna cried a lot. She cried when she was sad. She cried when she was happy. And she cried when she was angry, which she was now. It was a Donna thing.

I knew she was right. *I would be better off with her at my side.* She was cool-headed in a fight and a deadly shot. And she'd already been in a firefight with Rajnack back on Earth, when they had invaded her mother's farm. My chances of getting back alive were much better with her than without her.

But her chances of getting dead were also much better with me, and I had to think of her first. I shook my head. "I don't want you down there with me. It's too dangerous. I don't want you getting hurt. Or worse."

"I don't want you getting hurt either. That's why I'm going with you!"

"Forget it. This is my op, and we do things my way. I'm going alone and that's that!"

She got up and pushed by me to the door. "Fine. I can stay here, and help Montclair collect your body afterwards." The metal door banged when she slammed it behind her.

Montclair looked at me. "She didn't really mean that, I'm sure."

"I know. She's just worried about me."

"No, not that. I meant, if you get yourself killed, we won't be coming down to collect your body. We'll get out of here as fast as possible."

"Oh, right. Of course."

There was a moment of awkward silence. I didn't know what he was thinking but my mind was working further along the lines of my very probable death. "Seriously, though," I said. "If something happens to me down there, or you don't get my signal within seventy-two hours, don't come looking for me. Get out of here and take Donna home. You've already done enough."

"Of course, Jack," he said. "Now, let's get to the escape pod."

∞

Monty and I left the flight deck and headed down the narrow corridor towards the back of the ship. We passed the galley, and through the open door I saw Donna inside making coffee.

We made eye contact and she glared coldly at me for a moment before slamming the door shut. Gurth was nowhere in sight, and it didn't occur to me until later that it should have been a cause for concern.

Monty brought me down to the lower deck and we stopped in front of a round hatch. He opened it to reveal a spherical interior with four chairs, arranged in a circle facing inwards. The pod wasn't much larger than the seating. I'd used stalls in men's washrooms that were bigger.

"This is the escape pod. I've already programmed it to land in the hills about a mile from the Rajnack ship," Monty said.

The thought of dropping a hundred miles to the planet below in a tiny steel ball made my stomach queasy. "Why can't you fly me down?" I asked.

"We're too big, they'll see us," Monty said. "And we're transmitting on the transponder, remember? It will look suspicious if we drop to the surface a mile from the spaceport and then pop back up into orbit. That will attract attention, and we don't want that. Right now they think we are just another friendly ship in orbit. Let's keep it that way."

Monty continued, making it sound like a walk in the park: "It's simple. You drop down to the surface while it's still night. The pod won't register on their radar and I've turned off its locator beacon. It's night on that side of the planet, so you should be able to get down undetected. Wait for morning and make your way to the hills overlooking the spaceport. You'll need to wing it from there, depending on what you find."

"How do I fly this back once I have Johnnie?" I asked.

"You won't. These pods are strictly a one-way trip. Once you have Johnnie, call me on the radio and I'll come get you."

We went inside the tiny pod and he showed me how to operate it. There wasn't much to it, really. Secure the hatch, push the right buttons to release the pod from the ship, and enjoy the ride down. Internal guidance systems take over from there. I didn't have to know how to fly it. It came with a radio. It was a hand-held thing that looked like a 1980's style cell phone, and he took a few moments to show me how to use it.

Then Monty took me to an equipment locker and showed me some toys I might find useful on the surface. My favorite was a rocket pack that strapped to your back.

"This may help you get around down there," he said. "The gravity on the planet is light." He showed me how the controls worked, but there was no time to take it outside to practise. I'd have to learn quickly once I was on the surface.

We grabbed a backpack, extra ammo, water and food, and he helped me carry everything to the pod.

"We have to be quick," Monty said as we stood outside the pod door. "There are only a couple hours left until morning. Load the pod with whatever weapons you want to bring, and then get yourself strapped in. I'm going back up to the command deck to maneuver the ship into the orbit we will need."

Montclair disappeared up the ladder. The weapons locker was on the main deck. I was already familiar with Montclair's store of weapons, and I carried what I wanted down to the pod. I also decided to bring a universal translator with me. You never know.

I got all the gear into the pod and safely stowed away into lockers. Then I shut the hatch, made sure it was secure, and strapped myself into a seat. The controls for the pod were built into the arm of the chair. All I had to do was push two buttons at the same time and the pod would be ejected from the ship.

I toggled a switch to open the com to the command deck. All I got was the hissing of an open circuit. "Montclair. I'm strapped in and ready to go."

No answer.

I toggled the switch again. "Montclair, can you hear me? I'm ready to go."

The only answer I got was more static. "Monty? Donna? Can anyone hear me?"

And then came gunshots and Donna screamed through the open mic, and the ship jolted and tipped dangerously.

CHAPTER THIRTEEN

I UNSTRAPPED MYSELF, GRABBED A HANDGUN from one of the lockers and stuffed it into the back of my jeans. Then I cycled the hatch open and left the pod. I went up the ladder quickly. The hatch from the lower deck opened onto the floor of the main deck. I heard Donna yelling as I opened it.

I stuck my head up through the floor hatch and looked down the corridor towards the front of the ship. Montclair lay face down, in the open door to the cockpit. His body kept the door open.

Gurth was trying to pull Montclair's body out of the doorway, but with little success since he was forced to do it with one hand. His other hand held a gun pointed to the side, at something out of view inside the cockpit.

I couldn't see her, but I could hear Donna yelling. "Gurth, don't do this! This is crazy." She was in the cabin with Gurth.

Gurth kept his gun pointed to the left where Donna's voice came from and gave Montclair's arm another yank. I opened the hatch a little further but stayed on the ladder. Only my head was visible in the hatch.

"Gurth!" I shouted.

He swung the handgun towards me, and I quickly ducked and pulled the hatch closed. I listened for the shot, but nothing happened. I waited another couple of minutes, and then slowly stuck my head back up through the hatch and looked.

Montclair still lay across the threshold into the flight deck. Gurth was no longer in sight. I climbed out of the hatch onto the deck and pulled the handgun from the back of my pants. The weight of the metal felt reassuring in my hand. I went down the corridor quickly and stopped at the doorway in front of Montclair's body.

Donna sat in the co-pilots chair, looking at me wide-eyed. Gurth had squeezed in behind her, between her chair and the bulkhead. His shorter frame was well concealed behind her, and he held a gun at her head.

I slowly placed my gun down on the deck and showed him the palms of my hands. "Take it easy Gurth. We're all friends here."

"Don't try to stop me," he said without taking his gun off Donna.

"What's going on?" I asked.

"He wants to use the ship to attack the spaceport," Donna said.

"That's stupid Gurth. You'll just get us all killed."

"Better a glorious death regaining honour than your cowardly plan."

"Our plan is to rescue my son. You knew that from the beginning."

"Sneak in, sneak out, and strike no blow against the enemy! The way of cowards and weaklings."

"You're not thinking straight, fur brain. We talked about this, remember, and Montclair already told you this ship doesn't have the armaments. Even if we wanted to attack, we can't."

"I'm going to use an asteroid."

"And kill everyone down there, including Johnnie and thousands of innocent slaves."

He seemed to hesitate for a moment and looked down to the floor, as if he might re-think the idea. But when he answered, his voice took on a greater firmness. "I agree it's tragic, but the sacrifice is worth it."

"No one asked the slaves if they want to make the sacrifice."

"Sacrifices have to be made in the cause of the greater good. Don't try to stop me, or I'll be forced to shoot your female."

"And how are you going to fly this ship while holding a gun on Donna, not to mention keeping your eyes on us?"

He paused again, as if thinking something through for the first time. I had the impression that he was winging it, with no real plan thought out. While that gave him something to think about, I crouched down. Montclair was on the floor in front of me, and I felt for a pulse at his neck. I breathed a sigh of relief when I found one. But the pool of blood under him was growing.

I looked up at Gurth. "He's going to need medical attention quickly. Will you let me take him into the sick bay and stop the bleeding?"

He shook his head. "You're staying right here where I can see you."

"Then it seems we are at a bit of a standoff. Neither of us can move or do anything. You can't fly the ship like this, hiding behind Donna and holding a gun to her head. So what are you going to do?"

His whiskers twitched in thought, but he didn't say anything.

"I'm not going to stand here watching my friend bleed to death. I'm taking him to sickbay," I said.

"Move, and I shoot Donna."

"Is that your idea of honour?"

"It's not my first choice, but I will if you force my paw."

"Shoot Donna, and there's nothing left between you and me. You'll have a very angry and well-armed man loose on the ship. How far do you think you'll get?"

I wasn't bluffing either. I was in the doorway, and could roll backwards quickly, before he could get a second shot off. Then I'd get down to the armaments room and take my pick of heavy caliber weapons. There was even a long tube thing for launching rockets. With Donna dead, I'd gladly ram one of those things down his throat in the control room. Without Donna or Montclair to fly the ship, I had no hope of rescuing Johnnie anyway.

And I think Gurth saw it in my eyes. But I didn't move. He'd shot Montclair and he was crazy enough to shoot Donna and I didn't want it to come to that.

"What's it going to be, Gurth? Are we just going to stand here until our orbit decays and we burn up in the atmosphere? Because neither of us can move."

He was silent for a moment, whiskers twitching in thought. He couldn't fly the ship with us in the cabin, but he couldn't afford to let me out of his sight either.

One option was to just kill us, but even if he was Machiavellian enough to do that, he'd only manage to kill Donna before I got out of the way and drew my weapon. He'd be trapped in the cabin with me free to roam the ship.

"There's a way out of this Gurth, for all of us. And one that retains honour."

His whiskers twitched. "How?"

"There is no honour in this, for any of us. Where is the honour in friends killing each other while the enemy lives? Let's work together."

"We are not friends, Jack."

"We have a proverb on my world. 'The enemy of my enemies is my friend.' We accepted you as a comrade in good faith. And now you betray our trust."

Gurth growled back: "You betrayed me with your cowardly plans that would leave my enemies alive, and my family unavenged!"

"Gurth, listen to me. Donna and I are not cowards. We have both faced and killed Rajnack before, and I would gladly do it again. But there is no honour in your plan. We do not find any honour in killing innocent lives, and I cannot let you do this."

"Then how can we work together?" He asked.

I deliberately chose my words to appeal to his sense of honour. "Work with us. Help us rescue my son. Then we will take you back to your world and you'll live to fight another day. That will allow you to plan for revenge against the Rajnack properly, in a way that will not get you and thousands of innocent slaves killed. But what you are attempting now is a suicide mission. There is no honour in it."

That seemed to reach him. While I had Gurth's attention, Donna had slowly slid her hand down the arm of the chair towards the controls. I could see what she was doing, but from his angle behind her, Gurth couldn't.

Donna had been learning a lot from Montclair during our weeks in space and had a real aptitude for flying the spaceship. Montclair even said the other day that Donna was almost ready to solo.

Embedded in the arms of each flight seat were controls and a joystick. The ship could be flown from both seats. I didn't know what she had in mind because I didn't know what the controls did that she reached for, but slowly she got her hand close enough to stretch a finger towards a button.

She paused, index finger poised over the button, and looked significantly at me. She raised an eyebrow as if to say, *get ready – here goes nothing*.

I could only hope she knew what she was doing as she stabbed her finger down.

The ship lurched violently, then swung wildly towards the left. If I'd been a nautical type, I would have known if it was portside or starboard. I never could keep that straight. To me, it was just left, and I was flung forward, towards Gurth and Donna.

The violent motion threw Gurth back and the gun came away from Donna's head. She was ready with her elbow, which she rammed back, hard into his furry face. At the same time she twisted around to bring her other arm up and reached for the gun.

Gurth, thrown off balance, arms flailing in the air, fired wildly. The shot went high and punched through the top of the cabin. The ship rocked and the planet surface out the window began spinning. Donna tried twisting to grab his arm but was thrown out of her seat. Gurth tumbled after her as I regained my balance and threw myself towards him.

Air started hissing through the hole in the cabin. Fortunately it was a small calibre shot, so the hole was small. I got a hand on his arm and pushed it away just as he fired again, punching another hole in the cabin, this time through a side wall. I brought my other arm around and punched him with a couple of hard, rapid shots to his furry head.

His grip on the gun relaxed and I knocked it out of his hand as the ship continued to spin. Montclair's body fell onto the side wall as the ship spun, and I got a sight of the planet below careening wildly, which didn't do much for my stomach.

I shouted at Donna to grab the gun while Gurth and I tumbled around the cabin. Donna had fallen into the other seat, and lay straddled across its back, grabbing for something to hold onto as the ship kept spinning. She fell out of the seat against the bulkhead but managed to grab onto the back of the chair with one hand. With the other hand she stabbed at the controls on the console, then grabbed the joystick on the arm of the chair.

Gurth and I tumbled some more, but I definitely had the advantage with my larger size and longer arms. I used the leverage of my body to get on top of him and pin him against the bulkhead we ended up on. His short arms couldn't reach me, and they flailed uselessly in the air.

I couldn't see the gun and I yelled at Donna to grab it. But she had a better idea and pulled herself into the pilot's seat, strapped in, and began fighting the joystick with one hand while she stabbed at the controls with the other.

The spinning planet out the windows slowed as Donna stabilized the ship, and I slid off the bulkhead to the floor with Gurth on top of me. He managed to claw my face before I gave him another three or four rapid blows to his head, and he went limp.

The ship stopped spinning. Air hissed out from the cabin, and Montclair had fallen between the co-pilots seat and the jump seat behind it, bleeding profusely.

He was going to die soon if I didn't stop that bleeding, and we were all going to die of decompression if we didn't get the air leak plugged quickly.

I gave Gurth another hard punch in the face for good measure, not only because he'd annoyed me, but I also wanted to make sure he was out of commission for a while so Donna and I could take care of some urgent business before we all ended up dead.

CHAPTER FOURTEEN

AS SOON AS THE SHIP WAS STABLE Donna unstrapped herself from the captain's seat and ran aft. "I'm going for patches," she shouted as she raced down the corridor. With Donna taking care of that, the next priority was Monty. But I had to make sure Gurth didn't wake up and cause more trouble.

I briefly thought of putting him out the airlock. And then I spotted my handgun lying on top of a control panel where it had last fallen once the ship stopped spinning. A bullet to his head would save us all a lot of trouble.

It was tempting, and I thought about it for a minute. But I couldn't do it. I don't care what planet you're from, it didn't seem right. So I took my belt off and used it to tie his arms tight behind his back. Then I shoved him into the jump seat behind the co-pilots seat and strapped him in. I pulled the straps good and tight. With his arms tied behind his back he wouldn't be able to unstrap himself.

The jump seat is where I normally sat. They didn't have any controls, so even if Gurth came around he wouldn't be able to reach anything. I decided that should hold him long enough to get Monty down to the medical pod.

I carefully picked Monty up. His small frame in this low gravity was very light in my arms, and I had little trouble carrying him down the hall. I passed Donna on her way back to the cabin with packages in her arms.

∞

The medical pod was a fully automated robotic doctor. Monty's people, for all their love of brass and wood and spaceships that looked like they might have been powered by steam, really had some very advanced technology.

I laid him on the table, pulled the clear plastic lid down over him, and pushed the start button. The medical system took over from there.

The pod filled with gas to anesthetize him while lights from scanners tracked up and down his body, quickly identifying the problem. Robotic arms extended and got right to work, removing the bullet and stitching him up. This was a simple operation for the pod. It was quite capable of very advance surgery as well.

There was nothing for me to do so I went back up front. Donna had one hole sealed when I got back and was standing in the captain's chair and stretching up to reach the ceiling, where she stuck a square piece of material over the second hole. Then she applied silicon from a tube around the edges of the patch. The patches were kept on hand for quick repairs to holes caused by small rocks and meteorites that can be encountered in space. But they also came in handy for bullet holes.

When Donna finished sealing the second hole she said: "That will hold us until we get to a friendly port where permanent repairs can be made."

"That was some nice flying, sweetie," I said.

She turned around and looked at me. "How's Monty?"

"He was still alive when I laid him in the medical pod. The system told me he's expected to live."

"Good. If he dies, we're going to be lost in space for a long time."

"I don't know. You looked like you knew what you were doing."

"Sure, but navigating all the way back to Earth is an entirely different matter. Let's hope we don't have to find out the hard way."

I looked out the windows at the planet below. "Do you think you could manage taking this baby down to the surface?"

"I don't know. Why?"

"I think Monty will be all right, but he'll be out of commission for a while. Meanwhile, I'm heading down to the surface, and I'll need you to pick me up once I've found Johnnie."

The look on her face was not confidence inspiring. She took a big breath. "I don't know honey."

"Right now you're the best pilot we have."

"Maybe we should wait until Monty's better."

"We don't have the time. That Rajnack ship might not stay over for long. Maybe it just stopped for a quick re-supply before taking off again. We can't wait."

Gurth started to stir and I looked over at him. His eyes opened and he looked around, disoriented, then strained his arms against the straps. "May as well relax, Gurth. You're not going anywhere."

"Now that you've gained the upper hand, you will no doubt carry through with your cowards plan," he grumbled.

I realized I still had a problem. I couldn't leave him here with Donna. That was too risky and she was already in enough danger, and the last thing she needed was to worry about a crazy over-sized rabbit on board. Nor could I bring myself to just shoot him outright.

"Save your breath. I have to get to the surface and look for my son, and I can't leave you here with Donna. So I figure I'll take you with me. You can't do too much damage down there, and it'll give you an opportunity to kill Rajnack. What do you say?"

"I could kill more from up here," he spat back.

"That's not one of the options on tonight's menu. So it's either come down to the surface with me, or I'll put you out the airlock. Which will it be?"

∞

In the end he saw sense, not that he had much choice. I wasn't kidding about the airlock and I half hoped he'd test me on that. But I brought him down to the escape pod, arms still tied tight behind his back, and got him strapped into a seat. After strapping him in I stood in the open pod door to say my goodbyes to Donna.

I put my arms around her and pulled her close. "I'll give you a call when I've found Johnnie. Just follow my radio signal down and pick us up, then we blast off for Earth and home."

She tightened her arms around me. "You have a way of making it sound so simple." She wasn't smiling.

I grinned and brushed a tear away from her eye. "How hard can it be? I find Johnnie, give you a call, and you come get me. No problem."

She laughed. "Right, easy as one-two-three."

"Seriously though. If anything goes wrong or you don't hear from me in seventy-two hours, get out of here. I don't want you getting into trouble. If a Rajnack ship shows up in orbit and comes for you, don't stick around, okay."

"I'm not going to abandon you."

"Well, hopefully it doesn't come to that. But if it does I hope Monty wakes up and makes you do the sensible thing." Then I kissed her before she could answer and pulled pod door closed. The hatch sealed shut and I strapped myself in. I'd already loaded the pod with everything, and all I had to do now was wait. I couldn't release the pod while Donna was in the bay.

Gurth glared at me. "Is that how humans say goodbye to their mates?" There was derision in his voice.

I looked at him. "What do you guys do? Rub ears?"

"Our parting words are much longer, as befitting the importance of the relationship."

"Listen, we're on a bit of a time constraint here. Sorry if we didn't sing opera to each other."

He just snorted at me.

"Are you going to be grumpy like this the entire trip? Because the airlock is still an option."

Donna's voice crackled over the intercom before Gurth and I could continue with any further rapport. "I'm in the flight deck dear. Pod bay is clear. Ready when you are."

"See you in a few hours honey," I said, and pushed a button on the arm of my seat.

The mechanical locks holding us in the ship released with a series of pops and bangs, metal scratched on metal and filled our pod with what sounded like a giant dragging his fingernails over a long blackboard, and then suddenly dead silence as we fell into the void and tumbled through space.

The pod's internal systems quickly took over and stabilized us. We began to make a smooth and controlled descent to the surface. I watched our progress on a small monitor that flipped up from the seat's arm. Monty was right – I didn't have to worry about flying it. Which was just as well since I had no clue what to do.

Donna's voice came over the radio. "You're looking good dear."

"I bet you say that to all the guys," I said.

"I meant your flight path, goofball."

We hit some turbulence. "What's that?" I asked.

"You're entering the atmosphere. It might be a bit rough for a few minutes."

She didn't exaggerate. We shook violently for several minutes before it smoothed out. Then we fell silently for what felt like an eternity. The pod bumped hard once and then everything went still.

We were on the surface of the alien slave-world.

∞

I turned on the outside monitors to have a look around and only saw inky black. Switching to infrared and thermal I scanned the area and found nothing but a single warm-blooded animal of some kind, with six legs and about the size of a cat.

Gurth looked on with sullenness in his eyes. "What are you going to do with me?" He asked.

"I haven't decided yet, but it will go better for you if you keep your yap shut," I snapped.

He opened his jaw slightly as if to say something, then thought better of it and closed it again.

I remained in the pod and kept a watch on the surrounding area, wishing I'd thought to bring a thermos of strong coffee. There weren't even any peanuts on this flight. About forty-five minutes later, with no sign of pursuit, it seemed safe to conclude that we'd reached the surface undetected.

Monty had told me the escape pod wouldn't show on their radar. Now all I had to do was wait for morning light. I got out of my seat and wished again for that thermos of coffee.

"When are you going to release me?" Gurth asked while I was collecting things. I ignored him and packed a backpack with a radio, water and extra ammo. But I'd been giving that question a lot of thought: what to do with the half-rabid fur-ball.

I'd brought him with me because I didn't like the idea of leaving him in the ship with Donna. I was afraid it would put her in too much danger, and I didn't want her to have to worry about it. The ship didn't have a cell or any room we could keep him safely locked up. I could have tied him to something, I suppose, but in the back of my mind I'd be worried about him getting loose.

Maybe I should have just put him out the airlock and been done with it, but that wouldn't have been right, either.

The monitors showed the sky outside was getting lighter. It was time to go.

I finished packing. Into the backpack went the radio, water, food rations, extra ammo and the portable rocket pack. I already had a large knife on my belt. I strapped a universal translator to my shoulder just in case I met slaves that didn't speak English.

The weapons came next. I strapped a Winchester across my chest, and two shoulder harnesses held large caliber pistols. One was a traditional projectile firing device with a long barrel and curved wooden handle. The other was an energy weapon that fired a narrow, highly focused beam of energy. I called it a laser gun but Montclair had tried to correct me at one point. It didn't use light, he tried to explain. I didn't much care – laser gun worked for me.

There were also a couple of long barrelled rifles, one fired an energy beam and the other a large caliber projectile. I set them by the hatch. There was also a machinegun and a bazooka, but I left those. I couldn't carry everything.

I put on my coat and pulled a wool cap over my head. The coat was long and heavy for protection from the cold. Then I pushed the button to unlock the hatch and it made a hissing noise. I grabbed the handle and rolled it away. Cold air blasted against my face.

Gurth, seeing what I was about to do, struggled against the straps holding him in the chair. "You can't just leave me here!" He screeched.

I stopped in the hatch, halfway outside, and looked back at him. "Would you rather I shoot you? Because that's the only other option. I can't take you with me, can I? I'd have to take you handcuffed because I can't trust you, and I can hardly look for Johnnie and be worried about keeping an eye on you too. I don't see that working very well."

"What will you do?"

"I don't see that you have much to complain about, fur-brain. You shot Montclair, and I'm still angry enough to put a bullet in your head."

"I was sorry about Montclair. My intention was to wound him, you know. I didn't want to kill him. I'm a good shot – if I'd wanted to, I could have killed him."

"You almost managed to get us all killed with the decompression in the cabin. And Montclair lost a lot of blood."

"Will he be all right?" The note of concern in his voice sounded genuine and caught me off guard.

"Yes, the medi-pod told me he'd need a few days to recover, but he'll be all right."

"I'm glad to hear it."

I glared at him, momentarily wondering at his scrambled brains. Then I went outside. I put my head in the open door and said: "Sit tight. We'll be back to get you before we leave this rock, once I've found Johnnie."

He started to say something, but I pressed the button to close the hatch. I put him out of my mind and turned towards the task at hand: locating Johnnie on this barren piece of rock.

∞

I stood on the damp rock, watching the morning light spread across the surrounding waste. I could see my breath in the air. The light was diffused by a thick morning mist and grey clouds hung heavy in the sky above. Tall grasses and shrub clung to life in a thin layer of topsoil on top of the rock. About two miles distant a long ridge of rock pierced the horizon. The spaceport was on the other side of the ridge. The wall of the ridge looked steep and jagged.

I had water, rations, a rocket-pack, and enough guns and ammo to start a small war in Africa. With all the crap I was carrying it was a good thing the gravity on this rock was low.

I took my first step and almost launched myself into orbit. I sailed up into the air and then slowly fell back to the ground. Monty had warned me about the low gravity. I looked at the rock wall and thought that maybe getting up it wouldn't be so hard after all.

I moved across the ground easily, in long gliding steps, and covered the distance to the ridge quickly. I reached the base of the ridge and looked up at the jagged rock face. The black wet rock rose a good couple hundred feet. I slid the backpack from my shoulders and took out the rocket-pack.

It wasn't, technically speaking, a rocket, because it didn't use flame or rocket fuel. Instead, it discharged a compressed gas to create thrust. It worked well in orbit and on low gravity planets.

But I'd always wanted a rocket-pack as a boy. What kid didn't. This was close enough for me. I pulled the rocket-pack onto my shoulders and strapped it on. A metal armature curved around my waist that held the throttle and joystick.

Monty had explained how the controls worked in theory, of course, but there wasn't the room in his spaceship to take it for a practice spin.

I turned the rocket-pack on, looked up at the sky above, and pushed the throttle forward ever so gently. Air hissed out the back, but I didn't move. I kept pushing the throttle and slowly my feet lifted from the ground. I went up ten feet or so, then throttled back slowly and lowered myself to the ground. Then I did it again and played with the joystick to fly around in circles until I felt comfortable with the controls.

I felt ready. I tied a strap from the backpack to a leg, took a deep breath and throttled up, slowly rising into the air. I kept going straight up, passing by the rock face, rising hundreds of feet in the air.

Look! It's a bird! It's a plane! It's Super Jack!

I reached the top of the cliff and thumbed the joystick forward until I was in from the edge a few feet, then eased back on the throttle until my feet touched the ground.

The ground cover was better up here. A thick forest of large tree-sized plants stretched as far as I could see in both directions. The trunks looked impossibly thin and rubbery, supporting branches with huge, fern-like leaves. The soil felt loamy under my feet and was covered in dead leaves. The spaceport should be about a mile on the other side of the forest.

I took off my jetpack and hid it under some dead leaves. There wasn't enough pressure left in the tanks to get more than another five minutes of flight. Not enough to be useful when I got Johnnie.

I took the radio out of the backpack and switched it on. "Donna?"

Some hissing, then: "Hey Jack."

"I'm at the woods next to the spaceport."

"Be careful dear."

"Always. Over."

I double checked my weapons and pulled the backpack onto my shoulders. Then I ran into the forest of huge fern-like trees, holding the automatic in my hands, combat-ready. The likelihood of bumping into an unfriendly alien increased as I got closer to the spaceport.

In moments like this I was glad for my army training and two tours in Afghanistan. I just never in my wildest dreams thought I'd be using these skills against enemy aliens on a distant planet.

The ground was soft and I picked my way carefully, making as little noise as possible. The thick undergrowth and huge wide leaves made for limited visibility. I kept my eye on the sun shining through the tree-tops to keep my bearings. It was all too easy to get turned around and start wandering in circles in dense woods like these.

There seemed to be very little wildlife on this world. I'd seen no birds, and little evidence of animal life. My monitors last night had picked up only one animal.

Gurth told us this planetoid had recently been terra-formed from a dead rock to a world with an atmosphere that could support life. I wondered idly how the animals got here. Maybe escaped from ships, the way rats had been introduced to North America from European ships in port.

This went on for the longest time. I started to think that I should be getting to the spaceport clearing when something large moved to my left. I stopped and got low behind a tree.

Whatever the thing was, it made no attempt to hide itself. It moved noisily, leaves shaking, and I was pretty sure it hadn't heard me. The leaves from a tree not twenty feet away moved aside and a large Rajnack stepped into view.

He, or more likely she, was big even for a Rajnack. It wore a black suit of some kind and did not appear armed, probably because it thought it was in friendly territory.

I stayed low and out of sight, hoping to let it simply pass without any drama. There was no point in alerting others in the vicinity with unnecessary shooting. But it stopped not too far in front of me and sniffed at the air.

She took several large, deep snorts, then turned towards me. Apparently the Rajnack have a keen sense of smell, to go along with their monstrous size and musculature. Who knew?

She started pushing its way through the foliage towards me. I fired a single shot to the head and the large caliber did a nice job of putting her down. She fell forward with a thud.

I stayed where I was, listening for any indication that she had other girlfriends nearby. The woods around me were perfectly still, and after several minutes I came out of hiding and slowly approach the fallen Rajnack. She lay face down on the ground, half her head gone.

She wouldn't be any more trouble and I resumed my walk towards the spaceport. A few minutes later the trees ended at the edge of a large clearing. The clearing was round and indented, like a bowl in the ground. Probably an old meteor crater. Tufts of grass grew up from cracks in the smooth rock surface. And in the middle of the crater sat the Rajnack ship we'd been following all the way from Earth.

It had an aerodynamic design, light silver in colour with distinctive markings on the side. I crouched behind the wide trunk of a tree and set my gun down. Then I pulled a pair of binoculars out of my jacket and looked at the ship's markings. They were the same markings.

Monty had told me the markings were the name of the ship. Rajnack named their spaceships just like we named our ocean-going ships and space probes. He'd even translated it for me. It meant *Mother of Revenge.*

Such a charming sentiment, I thought as I looked at it. But I had the right ship. It had open doors at the back with a ramp extending down to the ground. I hoped Johnnie was still on it. My stomach got sick as I thought about the possibility he wouldn't be. And if he wasn't, and they'd dropped him off somewhere, I wouldn't even begin to know where to start looking.

I looked carefully around the area. There were only two other Rajnack ships on the ground. Black, football shaped, covered in bumps. They looked like overripe avocados, just like the one hidden in Beatrice's cabbage patch back home. Beyond them sat a series of low, squat buildings arranged around a tall metal structure that looked like an antenna array. The forest extended around the crater to the other side.

Rajnack moved slowly on the ground around the ships. A road came out of the woods on the far side and hugged the crater wall in a steep grade down to the bottom. Something moved along the road and I used my binoculars for a closer look.

A couple of small, wheelless vehicles glided down the slope. They floated a foot or so off the ground, like hovercraft. They had flat beds at the back onto which were strapped large crates. The front of each vehicle held a covered crew cab, with doors but no glass. Someone sat in the crew cab, who at this distance appeared to be very human. I assumed they were driving.

Gurth had told us that this planetoid was used as a resupply station for the mining colonies in the nearby asteroid belt. It was also used as a home and headquarters for the Rajnack rulers. And according to Gurth they even grew food here for the mining colonies. It made sense to have a nearby food source.

Crates were stacked on the ground around the Rajnack ship, and more human slaves carried crates up into the ship. It looked like the Rajnack were re-supplying the *Mother of Revenge.*

What I needed was a way to get close to it undetected, and watching the hover-trucks gave me an idea. The vague outline of a plan began to take shape in my mind, and I started walking. I'd work out the details as I made my way around the lip of the crater.

CHAPTER FIFTEEN

IT TOOK THE REST OF THE MORNING, but I reached the other side of the rim wall where the road entered the crater. I stayed away from the edge, just inside the tree line to use as cover so I wouldn't be spotted from below. I didn't encounter any more Rajnack in the woods and I hoped that the friends or shipmates of the one I'd killed wouldn't start to miss her too soon.

The road was empty when I reached it. It wasn't much more than a strip of smooth rock cutting through the woods. I got myself hidden in the foliage next to the road and waited.

The outlines of a plan were taking shape in my mind. The main idea was to commandeer one of the hovercrafts and use it to drive up to the *Mother of Revenge* sitting in the spaceport below. I'd approach slowly and hope that any guards that saw me would assume I was just one of the slaves delivering cargo. I'd been watching hovercraft all morning do exactly that.

I hoped that would let me get close enough. Then I'd pick up a crate and walk up the ramp. Maybe that would work. Maybe I'd have to shoot my way in. I'd have to play it by ear depending on how the Rajnack guards reacted.

If my plan worked I'd be able to get inside the ship, where I hoped to find Johnnie. I was also gambling that there wouldn't be many crewmembers inside because they were in port.

It wasn't long before a vehicle appeared in the distance, gliding silently towards the crater. The cab of the hovercraft was open, and the driver looked very human. He wore bright orange coveralls and had a thick ring around his neck. Gurth had told us the Rajnack took slaves from many races, including mine. So far, everything he said had checked out. There were no Rajnack in sight. Apparently they weren't too worried about slaves escaping on this rock, and when you thought about it, it made sense. Where would they run?

I turned on my translator and inserted the earbud. Even if they were human, it didn't mean they spoke English. And I was better with the alien Radauti language than French or Spanish, although I could manage a *Guten Tag* for my German speaking friends.

As the truck approached I slid down the short slope and stepped out into the middle of the road to block the way. I unslung my weapon, although I did not point it directly at the driver. I held up a hand and shouted: "Stop!"

He looked startled and stopped the vehicle. He had pale white skin with long blonde hair sticking out from his cap. The truck bobbed in the breeze as it floated a foot from the ground.

"Hello friend," I said. "I'll be needing that truck."

"Wo kommen sie heir? Wer bist du?"

Crap, German. I made an adjustment on the translator.

"Get out of the truck," I said, gesturing with my Winchester. I hoped the bluff worked. I actually had no idea what I'd do if he didn't, since I had no intention of shooting him. The German's face turned thoughtful, and he did not appear nearly as frightened as I'd hoped.

He took in my clothes and the Winchester in my hands. "Who are you? You're not a prisoner. How did you get here?"

I switched off my translator. "You speak English," I said.

"Yes, of course. I'm from Germany. Most Europeans speak English and at least one or two other languages. You sound American."

Why do foreigners always think that? "Canadian, actually. But considering the distance we're both from Earth, you and I are kissing cousins. Now, I'd hate to shoot a fellow Earthling, but I really do need that truck." I gestured with the rifle for him to get down.

He climbed out and stood on the ground. I got into the cab. The seat was a bench that stretched the entire width of the cab, and the controls were in the middle. I sat down and had a look at them. Three pedals on the floor, a tall joystick extending from the floor and a few buttons on the dash. Looked simple enough, I thought. How hard can this be?

I looked at the guy. He was way too skinny and his face was gaunt. He looked back at me with bright blue eyes from deep sockets. I didn't know how long he'd been here, but slaves can have the spirit beaten out of them after long periods of harsh treatment and abuse. I wondered what horrors he'd suffered at the hands of the Rajnack. I reached into an inside pocket and got out a chocolate bar, one of the last we'd packed before leaving Earth in a hurry. I tossed it down to him. "Here, you look like you could use this."

He unwrapped the Snickers bar and ate ravenously. "How many guards at the big silver ship?" I asked. There were only three ships parked in the crater, and the other two were the small black variety.

"Just one at the bottom of the ramp. There may be more inside, I can't say for sure. But I don't think so. I saw a large number of them heading into town after they landed."

That's all I really needed to know. There were more questions I wanted to ask, but I had to be quick in case more hovercraft came along, or worse, Rajnack.

He finished the chocolate bar and looked me over. "Who are you? How did you get here?"

"I'd love to stay and chat, but I'm in a hurry," I said, looking over the controls. How do I move forward? Press a foot pedal or use the joystick? I pushed the joystick gently forward, and the hovercraft shot backwards. I pulled back, and the truck stopped and went forward.

"Press the button on top of the stick to stop," the German shouted as I passed by.

I stopped the vehicle and bobbed in the air. The truck wobbled violently, and I fought with the joystick to steady it, but it wouldn't co-operate. The German came up beside the cab and looked at me. "You don't know what you're doing. You'll never make it down the road into the crater. It's a sheer drop. You'll crash this and kill yourself, if the Rajnack don't get you first."

"I don't see that I have much choice but to try and hope for the best," I said.

"Yes you do. Let me drive."

I shook my head. "I don't know."

"Listen, Dummkopf, driving the truck like that, the Rajnack will see you coming a kilometer away and know something's wrong. These hovercrafts are extremely difficult to handle. But with me driving, you have a chance at getting to the ship without them suspecting anything."

"Why would you do that?"

"You came from Earth, correct? You must have a spaceship."

I nodded. "It's in orbit, waiting for my signal."

"Take me back to Earth with you."

I looked into his half-starved face. He looked frail, but a fire burned in his eyes and his face was strong. "You realize there is a good chance we'll both be caught, or worse, killed," I said.

"Then why are you doing this?" He asked.

I motioned with my head towards the crater. "They have my son down there, in that ship."

"Then I understand why you do this. What father wouldn't? I will help you, and all I ask is that you take me with you."

"We might be killed," I repeated.

"There are worse things than death," he said. "And for a chance to be back home, I will happily risk it. There is no hope for prisoners here. They use us up and then, when our bodies are no longer strong enough to be of service, they eliminate us and discard us like garbage. I've been here long enough to know what happens."

I didn't answer right away, thinking it through. I didn't know if I could trust him. What if he chose to betray me in an attempt to ingratiate himself to the Rajnack?

"You must make up your mind quickly. Other trucks will be coming," he urged.

Looking into his eyes I could see his spirit, burning bright with passion and sincerity. I made my decision. "Hop in," I said, and shifted to the side.

He got behind the joystick and, with a touch, steadied the truck. Then he gently pulled back, so slightly that I could hardly see the stick move. The truck glided forward.

A few minutes later we reached the crater wall and came to a hairpin turn. I thought we were going to shoot right over the edge until he deftly steered the truck to follow the road down into the crater. I looked over the side, at the sheer drop below.

The German had been right. I never would have made that turn.

∞

I learned that his name was Eric. He'd been kidnapped by the Rajnack when he was nineteen, while hiking with friends in the Alps. They were brought here and put into forced labour. He was the only one of his group left alive.

We reached the crater floor and turned towards the silver ship. "What will we find when we get there?" I asked.

"There will be one guard at the bottom of the ramp," he said. "You need to take care of it quickly. Do you see this ring around my neck?"

I had noticed it and wondered what it was. "All he has to do is touch a button on his belt and my head goes 'poof'." He made a gesture with his hands around his head, to illustrate an exploding skull. "It is a very effective means of keeping prisoners in line."

"Any more Rajnack around," I asked. I was looking around but couldn't see any.

"Not many. They don't expect any trouble out here, and the crews go into town."

We got closer to the ship. It was a long, sleek cylinder with short wings and a pointed nose. Overall, about the size of a jumbo jet back home. The rifles were on the floor of the cab, out of sight. I slid a hand inside my jacket and gripped the handle of my Ruger 44. Despite the chilled air my palms were damp with sweat.

"Have you been inside that ship?" I asked.

He nodded. "Yes, helping load it."

"What can you tell me of the interior layout? Any idea where prisoners are held?"

"Of course. I was brought here as a prisoner myself, in a ship just like it. The ramp will take you into a cargo area. There is a corridor down the middle going towards the front, where the control cabin is. About halfway down the corridor you will come to a set of circular stairs. Take them down. When you get to the bottom, go left, towards the rear again. The prisoners are held in a room at the back, under the cargo hold. If your son is on board, you should find him there."

We pulled up to the ship. The huge bulk of the Rajnack, almost eight feet tall, dwarfed the humans around her. There were also a few prisoners from Gurth's race. They were shifting crates around and carrying them up the ramp. The Rajnack didn't seem to notice us until we slid to a stop at the bottom of the ramp. Then she turned and gazed at us.

I was not dressed, like the prisoners, in a bright yellow or orange jumpsuit. She may have had a moment to wonder why I wore different clothes, but I didn't give her the time to consider the significance of it. I brought out my handgun and pumped two quick shots through her head. She tumbled over face first.

The prisoners on the ground stopped what they were doing and stared at me. "Keep the engine running," I said to Eric and jumped out of the cab holding the handgun.

I ran up the ramp into the dark interior of the alien craft. A few prisoners milled around, shifting crates and strapping them in, seemingly oblivious to what had just happened outside. A few of them stopped to stare at me in surprise.

There was another Rajnack at the back of the cargo hold, blocking the way into the central corridor. She saw me and reached for a weapon clipped to a belt, but I had the advantage of surprise and shot first.

And missed. I ducked behind a crate, knocking over a large woman in yellow coveralls, just as the Rajnack took her shot. I moved to the end of the crate and came up, gun held out in front. She was visible above the other crates and I squeezed off two rapid shots. Her head exploded in a cloud of grey goo and she fell to the deck with a thud.

Two down. I wondered how many more were on the ship. I had to move fast. Right now I had the advantage of surprise – the Rajnack were clearly not expecting trouble and the sense of safety at being in their own port had made them complacent.

But as the shooting continued and the body count rose, the advantage of surprise would quickly evaporate. I didn't know if there were more Rajnack down the corridor, but if there were, they probably heard the shooting.

I raced down the corridor, my boots banging on the metal flooring. The metal walls were black and damp looking. I passed hatches and small open areas crammed with strange looking instruments and equipment. No more Rajnack appeared in the corridor. I came to the stairwell about half-way down, just as Eric described, and made a quick decision to keep going. I wanted to clear this level before going below, and possibly even disable the ship so it couldn't come after us when Donna came to pick us up.

The corridor ended at a closed hatch. I was at the front of the ship, according to Eric. This had to be the flight cabin. I put a hand on the latch and looked back. A small crowd of humans and a few of Gurth's rabbit-folk had gathered at the end of the corridor watching me.

I turned the latch and pulled. It didn't budge. I pushed. Nothing. But when I turned the latch the other way and pulled again, it swung open and I entered the cabin, gun first.

A single Rajnack sat in a chair in front of a huge console of blinking lights and instruments. Apparently, she hadn't heard the shooting through the closed door and was intent on the instruments in front of her when I entered. She pivoted her body to look at me, but Rajnack are slow at this because they have no necks and have to turn their entire body.

She didn't have a chance. One quick shot from my Ruger and her body slumped against the instrument panel. I quickly pumped a few more rounds into the instrument panel. I doubted the damage I inflicted was beyond repair, but spaceships are delicate machines and a few bullet holes through its instruments would be enough to ground this thing for a long while. They wouldn't be coming after us any time soon.

I ran back down the corridor to the applause of on-looking humans and came to the stairwell. The stairwell was wide, big enough to accommodate the Rajnack's girth. I reached the bottom quickly, taking the stairs two at a time. The corridor at the bottom was dark and narrow, lined with conduit and piping, damp with condensation. No bad gals in sight.

I made my way towards the back, where Eric said there should be a holding cell where the prisoners were kept. I came to a hatch and tried it. It wouldn't open. I banged on it, shouting Johnnie's name, and when no answer came I moved on to the next door.

There were several doors. Some of them opened, revealing small rooms that looked like equipment lockers. Others were used for storage. I kept working my way down, trying each door, banging on the ones that wouldn't open and calling out for Johnnie.

I hoped there weren't Rajnack on the other side of the doors. I was getting close to the end of the corridor and began to despair of finding him when I came to a locked door. I banged on it and called for Johnnie, and this time received an answer.

A small voice said, "Dad?"

"Johnnie! It's me!"

"Dad, is that really you?" He cried.

"Yes, it's Dad!"

"Dad, get me out of here!" His voice was weak and scared.

"I'm trying," I said and worked the latch. It wouldn't open. Being a prison cell, it would be locked. I stood in the corridor looking at the door and the walls around it, considering my next move.

There was no lock or keypad that I could see, but there was a flat glassy plate on the door next to the latch. I had an energy weapon, and thought about using it to blast the door, but I didn't know how big the room was, or whether Johnnie could move far enough away to be safe.

Maybe the prisoners knew how the Rajnack opened these locked doors. "Johnnie, sit tight. I can't open the door and I'm going to see if I can find a key."

"Okay Dad," he answered.

I ran back to the stairwell and took the stairs up two at a time. I came up through the hatch carefully, handgun drawn, in case more Rajnack were on the ship.

The small crowd of yellow clad prisoners, mostly human but some of Gurth's race, still milled around at the bottom of the ramp. A good sign, since they would probably have scattered if more Rajnack had shown up.

I ran to the top of the ramp. Eric was still there, waiting for me in the hovercraft. A tall woman grabbed my sleeve, saying something in desperate, rapid-fire Spanish. I switched my translator off. Another man pushed his way forward through the crowd to stand in front of me and spoke English with a heavy Australian accent. "You're from Earth, aren't you mate?"

I ignored him and shouted at Eric: "I found the prison cell. Do you know how to open the door? Do they use keys?" I was thinking I may have to search the bodies of dead Rajnack for keys.

The Australian was large and he shifted in front of me. "Listen mate, you have to take us with you. You must have a ship, right?"

Eric answered me from behind the Aussie's back: "They place their hands on a glass pad on the door. It only works for them."

The Australian grabbed my shoulders when I didn't answer. "Where's your ship? You have to take us with you."

I pushed his arms away. "Not now. I need to get my son out of here." I turned to go but a strong pair of hands grabbed my jacket. I drew my side arm and spun around, and held the gun up to his face. "Don't get in my way. I'm getting my son out."

"Take us with you," he pleaded. "Please!"

I looked around at the crowd looking at me with desperate eyes and gaunt faces. Several more stepped closer, despite the gun in my hand.

I'd already promised room on the ship for Eric, which I intended to keep. But even that was stretching it. No way could Monty's little ship hold all these people. It simply wasn't big enough, nor could its environmental systems handle the extra oxygen required or keep the air scrubbed of carbon dioxide. We'd all asphyxiate in space long before we made it home.

"Look, friend. I'd like to help, believe me…" I started to say, when Eric interrupted. "Jack, we've got company. You'd better be quick."

I looked up and a handful of Rajnack came running towards us from the cluster of buildings. I'd been lucky so far. But of course, it was only a matter of time before the disturbance drew attention. Then I noticed smoke billowing across the ground, carried by the breeze from the front of the ship. Apparently, I'd caused an electrical fire with my shots in the cockpit, and the front of the ship was burning.

"How do I open the door, then?" I asked Eric. He shook his head and looked nervously at the approaching Rajnack.

But the Australian's eyes narrowed. "You're going to have to use one of their hands, mate. The doors only open at their touch."

A gruesome thought occurred to me. Of course. The glass panels were hand scanners for controlled access. They didn't have to enter a passcode, just touch the pad. I thought quickly. The Rajnack in the cockpit was likely a pilot, which I guessed would make her a senior officer. And senior officers would have access to the entire ship.

I ran back to the cockpit. The body was still slumped over in the chair. I took out a knife from my belt, swallowed hard, and used it to hack off her large, clawed hand. It was bloody and stomach-turning work, but I had no choice.

I had to choke back the bile rising in my throat, burning its way to my mouth, as I sawed off her hand. The bones were very tough and thick, and it took some hacking to get through, but the hand finally fell away and dropped to the floor. I picked up the severed hand and ran for the stairwell, took the stairs to the lower deck, raced down the dark corridor looking for the right door, and slapped the clawed hand against the glass panel.

Something hissed, I turned the latch and pushed. The door swung in and my son stood in the corner of the small room.

Chapter Sixteen

HE STOOD IN THE CORNER, STARING AT ME wide eyed. He'd lost some weight, but otherwise looked unharmed. The room smelled foul. It was a small, bare room without furniture. Not even a toilet. A pile of filth in one corner, urine puddled around it. Scraps of food littered the floor. They'd kept him locked up like an animal. Not even. Caged animals back home got better treatment than this.

"Dad!" He said weakly and rushed into my arms. I fell to my knees, throwing my arms around him, and started crying. "Johnnie," I said through my sobs.

He held me close. "I thought I'd never see you again," he said. And then the flood of tearful questions came. Confused and terrified, he needed to talk. But I had to shush him. "Later," I said. "We have to get out of here."

I forced myself into some measure of control. I thought of the Rajnack outside, running across the tarmac. It was probably already too late. I pulled the radio out of my jacket and thumbed the switch: "Donna, I found him."

A moment of hissing on the line, then: "Is he okay?"

"Yes, unharmed. I'm getting him out of the ship now."

"Wonderful news Jack. I've got your location locked. Keep your radio on. I'll follow the signal down to you."

"We'll be outside the silver ship. It'll be dicey. There are Rajnack outside, but I will try to take care of them before you land."

I'd have to take care of them. If they fired at our ship and damaged it, we'd all be stranded on this slave world and never get home.

Maybe all I'd managed was to get Donna and Montclair killed too. But if I could get outside and hold them off, long enough for Donna to land, and if we were quick, maybe we had a chance. A lot of 'ifs'.

And then howling that sounded like the depths of hell filled the corridor. Johnnie's eyes widened with terror. "It's them."

"And they sound really pissed," I said.

I checked my Ruger. Empty. I tossed it aside and pulled out one of Montclair's handguns, an energy-beam weapon. The drawback to these things was that the power pack was limited. It would only be good for three or four shots strong enough to kill. But it came with some handy settings.

Large thuds rang down the corridor, like boots hitting the steel floor. I set the handgun to fire a wide pulse and stuck my head around the door.

Two Rajnack filled the corridor, weapons drawn, moving slowly in their ape-like gait. One arm extended to the ground, the other holding a gun. A third one jumped into the corridor from the stairwell, landing with a thud.

The first one saw me and aimed. I pulled my head back inside the door just as her shot sizzled by and scorched the bulkhead. I swung around fast, arms out and fired down the corridor without needing to aim. The wide-range energy pulse swept down the corridor and fried the first two Rajnack. The third one, further back, took a shot at me as her girlfriends were collapsing to the floor. She didn't have time to aim and her shot went wide. I pressed the trigger again and fired off another energy pulse. There wasn't enough power left to kill her, but it knocked her down, stunned.

I dropped the energy gun, unsnapped the Winchester strapped across my chest, and ran forward. The alien moved slowly, groggy from the stun. I put a couple rounds into her and she stopped moving.

I stopped in the corridor, listening. Nothing else moved in the stairwell and there was no noise from the deck above. "Johnnie," I called. "Come quick."

He appeared at the door, saw me, then looked at the bodies on the floor. Their huge bulk filled the narrow passageway, blocking the way. I motioned with my hand, urging him on. "Quick!"

He ran and joined me. Whiffs of smoke rose from the blackened skin of the Rajnack and the smell of burnt meat filled the air. I lifted Johnnie up and over the first body, then jumped over myself. I did the same for the next two bodies and then we ran to the circular stairwell.

I stopped at the bottom to listen and placed an index finger over my lips for Johnnie to be quiet. When no sound came from above, I said to Johnnie: "Stay right behind me." Then I climbed the stairs, taking it slow, and when I was high enough I poked my head up through the opening in the floor just enough to look around. The passageway was clear in both directions. You could hear a pin drop.

I climbed up the rest of the way and Johnnie followed me. I stood in the corridor and pulled the radio out. "Donna, do you read me?"

"Yeah Jack."

"What's your ETA?"

Some static, then: "Nine minutes."

"Come on," I said to Johnnie, grabbed his hand with my left, and holding the Winchester in my right, we walked quickly down the passageway.

When we reached the top of the ramp I looked out across the tarmac. Bodies littered the ground outside. Most of them were human, clothed in yellow or orange jumpsuits. I spotted Eric lying among the dead, next to the big Australian who had pleaded with me. The Rajnack had slaughtered the slaves when they arrived here looking for me.

More Rajnack where running across the tarmac towards the ship. They spotted us at the top of the ramp, and several let out loud howls. Then they quickened their pace.

There was no place to go but back inside the ship. I grabbed Johnnie's arm and pulled him down the corridor with me.

"What are we going to do Dad?" Johnnie cried, his words tinged with terror.

"Find a place to hide," I said in a brave tone, knowing it was hopeless.

I took him all the way down the corridor, passing the stairwell to the lower deck, and went towards the cockpit. We reached the cockpit door, the end of the line, just as the first few Rajnack appeared at the top of the ramp.

I opened the door, pulled Johnnie in with me, then locked it. The bulky and quite dead Rajnack still slouched in the chair where I'd left her. I got Johnnie down on the floor behind the other chair, squatted on the floor in front of him, and drew my weapon.

I listened to the footsteps thudding towards us.

There were only two rounds left in the Winchester, not that it mattered one bit. I called Donna: "Where are you?"

"Three minutes out," she said.

"Turn around and go home," I said. "It's over."

She would be flying into a hail of weapons fire. I was trapped and had no chance of getting out. I'd never reach her, and she couldn't do anything for me.

"What are you talking about?"

"I can't get out Donna. And you can't reach me and will get yourself shot down if you get any closer."

A moment of static on the line, then: "Just hang on Jack. I'm almost there."

"Turn around," I yelled.

More static. Then, simply: "No."

Tears wet my eyes. "You'll just get yourself killed. There's nothing you can do."

"I can see the spaceport now. Where are you?"

"Trapped inside the cockpit, with several angry Rajnack outside the door. I can't get out. I'm sorry Donna. I guess I put you through all this for nothing. But at least you and Monty can get away alive."

The line was quiet for a few seconds, then some static, and then: "Two minutes out."

I wanted to swear at her, but a dread voice from outside the door spoiled the moment. "Jack... Winters...we meet again. You have surprised me. I didn't think human worms had it in them."

The voice was slow and heavy, growling out each syllable dripping with malice.

"Let us go Rajnack," I yelled back, with the bravest sounding voice I could manage. "Let us go and I'll supply you with all the coffee you need. You'll be rich." Lame, I know, but what did I have to lose? Either that, or cry like a little girl pleading for my life.

"We are past that point now, human. But I do not wish to inflict any more damage on my ship than necessary, otherwise I could easily blow this door open, along with you inside. But that might cause unnecessary and expensive damage to my instruments. So I am prepared to negotiate this with you human. Open the door, and your deaths will be quick and painless."

I looked over at Johnnie and struggled to keep myself under control. He just stared at me with huge eyes, round with terror.

"And if I don't?"

"If you don't, and I am forced to damage my ship further to get inside, then I promise that I won't kill you...first. First, you will be made to watch your son die a very slow and horrible death, while I inflict unbearable pain upon him. Then, after your mind has been reduced to madness by the sight of this, I will kill you too, slowly."

I saw no way out, and the thought of Johnnie dying like that was too much to bear. I looked at him and fought back the tears. He looked back at me and sniffled. A sob choked his throat. "Dad, I'm scared."

I turned back to the door and struggled for a moment to get my emotions in check. Then I said to the door: "Tempting offer. Can I think it over?"

I was hoping to buy time, but I had no clue how I was getting us out of this.

"Human, you have no time and no options, you..."

Several loud bangs cut her off suddenly, followed by the cries of other Rajnack howling. More bangs, and then everything went completely silent.

I waited for a moment without moving. Then another voice, a familiar voice, broke the silence. Not of a Rajnack but from the chest of a much smaller creature, although not human.

"Jack, are you all right?" The voice said.

I pushed the door open. The corridor was filled with several dead Rajnack. And a bit further back stood Gurth, holding a large caliber Winchester and looking very pleased with himself.

∞

"Are you going to stand there gawking at me all day, or do you want to come along before more of these arrive?" He nodded his head towards the pile of bodies before him.

"Gurth?" I said dumbly.

"Yes, Jack. I believe we've already been introduced. Now stop looking at me like you've seen a ghost and come along quickly."

"But how did you…?"

"There's no time for that. Come along." He turned and started walking back to the ramp. He looked ready to start a one-man war. In addition to the Winchester in his hands, he had a bazooka slung over his back along with a rifle. It was the same bazooka I'd decided to leave in the pod. A bag hung across his back from the other shoulder.

I pulled myself together and grabbed Johnnie's arm and pulled him with me out of the cockpit. I had to lift him over the bodies of the dead Rajnack, and then we started running for the ramp.

We reached the ramp and ran down. Bodies still littered the ground outside, both human and Rajnack. Gurth was likely responsible for the additional Rajnack bodies when he fought his way into the spaceship.

I got the radio out of my backpack. "Donna, where are you?"

"Look up into the sky Honey. To your left."

I looked. A small bright dot, gleaming with reflected sunlight, moved through the sky towards us. It grew larger as I watched, and it became a brass bullet.

"I can see you at the bottom of the ramp!" Donna's voice cried joyfully through the radio.

I pointed for Johnnie's benefit. "That's Donna! We're going home!" Johnnie started jumping and waving and cheering.

Gurth said flatly: "We have company."

More Rajnack were running across the tarmac from the far side of the spaceport. They were a good mile away. I looked back at the approaching ship and tried to judge the timing. It was going to be very tight. Johnnie tugged on my sleeve. "Dad, look!"

I looked to where he was pointing, and one of the two smaller black ships was lifting from the ground. Donna wouldn't stand a chance.

"Gurth," I said. "Time to use that bazooka!"

He turned around and saw the black football rising into the air. He dropped his Winchester and got down on one knee. Then he unslung the bazooka and the bag from his shoulders. "There's two rockets in the bag, Jack," he said as he brought the bazooka up and set it on his shoulder.

I opened the bag and pulled out one of the rockets and inserted it into the back of the tube. Then I patted him on the back and stepped clear, pulling Johnnie with me.

Gurth knelt and looked through the eyepiece of the aiming site. I picked up the Winchester from the ground and fired off a few bursts towards the Rajnack.

I was too far away to be effective, but it would give them something to think about and slow them down. They fanned out to the sides and got down to the ground.

Flame sprouted from the back of the bazooka and the small rocket shot into the air, trailing white vapor. It arced to the right a bit to correct its course and closed with the target.

The ship was too close to the ground to take evasive action. It exploded in a plume of fire and smoke and black bits of debris rained onto the tarmac.

Pinging noises came from the ship's hull next to us and I realized the Rajnack must be shooting. "Get down," I said and pulled Johnnie to the ground with me.

I lifted my head a bit to look for our ship but couldn't see it. Then a large shadow passed overhead, and I craned my neck and looked straight up. The brass hull of Montclair's ship filled the sky, passed slowly over us, and lowered to the ground a few feet away.

It hovered a foot from the ground, its open airlock door inviting us in. Gurth lay on the ground a few feet away, his head facing the other way.

I got up and grabbed Johnnie by the arm. "Come on," I urged. He got up, I put an arm around his shoulder, and we ran for the airlock. When we reached the airlock I picked Johnnie up under the armpits and hoisted him inside. "Get in and lay down," I said. I watched him scramble further in.

Pinging noises came off the hull around me. The Rajnack had picked themselves off the ground and were running towards us. Gurth still lay on the ground.

"Gurth," I shouted. "Come on!" He stirred but did not get up. I went over to him and knelt at his side.

"Gurth, what's wrong?" Then I noticed the thick red liquid spreading out over the ground from under his body.

He rolled over and looked at me with weak eyes. "Go without me," he said. "Only leave me a weapon and I'll hold them off as long as I can."

Donna's voice reached me from the radio in my pocket. "Jack, are you in?"

I picked up the radio. "Johnnie is. Give me another minute."

"We don't have a minute!"

I set the radio down and slung the bazooka and ammo bag over a shoulder. Then I used both arms to lift Gurth up. "Jack, what are you doing?"

I started walking for the airlock. On Earth he would have weighed maybe a hundred pounds. With the weapons and ammo over my shoulder, it would have been difficult. But on this planetoid he was easy to carry. "Taking you with me."

"Just leave me. It will be a noble death. I've regained my honour and had my revenge. Let me die now, killing my enemies."

"Nothing doing. You'll live yet to fight another day," I said as I carried him over to the ship.

We reached the airlock. The inside door of the airlock was open as well, and Johnnie sat in the corridor watching us. I set Gurth down inside and then grabbed the handles at the sides and hauled myself up and in, shouting in a loud voice: "Donna, we're in. Go! Go!"

The floor of the ship tilted and slammed against me as I rolled inside the door. Outside the airlock the ground fell away rapidly and wind whipped inside. I slapped a button on the wall and the airlock door slid shut with a hiss.

Then I rolled over and lay on my back, breathing with relief. I started to get up when an invisible force slammed me back down, pressing me hard against the floor. Donna's voice came over the intercom: "Welcome aboard boys. Just sit tight while I put some distance between us and the bad guys."

For the longest while we could barely move. Gurth and I inside the airlock, Johnnie in the corridor just outside, G-forces pinning us to the floor as Donna kicked it into high gear.

CHAPTER SEVENTEEN

SPACE TRAVEL gives you a lot of time to think. The routine maintenance we all shared required maybe two hours out of every twenty-four. Behind its brass and wood nineteenth century décor, Monty's was a highly automated ship. Once we had it pointed in the right direction, there wasn't a whole lot to do until we arrived home.

During the long transit between worlds our biggest enemy was boredom.

But rescuing Johnnie was not the end of our problems, and these were the dark thoughts that troubled my mind while we sped through the eternal blackness of space. I couldn't see any way that Donna and I would be able to return to any semblance of our old lives. Just avoiding prison was going to be difficult.

Johnnie and I had lots of time to talk, and for the first few days he barely left my side. He was safe once again with Donna and I, and it didn't take long for him to relax and open up. We didn't do much but listen as he told us everything that had happened. He cried a lot at first and sometimes the words would come in a flood of emotion. Donna and I spent a lot of time in the lounge with him, letting him talk it out.

∞

We'd been in space for a couple of weeks. Montclair was up and about again, his wounded arm in a sling. The four of us sat in the galley after a meager dinner of tinned beans. We all still felt hungry, but the food had to be carefully rationed. For dessert, Montclair, Donna and I had coffees and Johnnie had one of the last tins of diced fruit. Gurth was still recovering in the medical pod, and it would be a few more days before he could join us.

"I still don't understand how we managed to escape," I said, in a deliberate attempt to distract my own mind from its dark preoccupations. "I mean, surely the Rajnack had better weapons. It is a wonder we didn't get blasted with rockets or energy beams or something. It should have been easy for them to take us out. But all they did was fire at us with small calibre projectile weapons."

Montclair stroked his beard. "I think the explanation is simple enough. They couldn't risk damage to their ship. You were too close to it. Think about it. They are on a very isolated colony. That ship was the only interstellar craft in port. They are also extremely expensive, and you two were, after all, very low priority targets. Johnnie is just a boy, an unimportant prisoner. You weren't worth the risk. The two small black ships that were in port at the time weren't capable of deep space flight. They might go months before another ship arrives."

"Well, they're still going to be stuck for a while. I pumped a few rounds into the instrument panel in the cockpit," I said with a smile.

"That would explain the lack of pursuit," Montclair said.

A few weeks into the trip home, Johnnie seemed to have talked enough about his ordeal at the hands of the Rajnack, and we started exploring the spaceship together. What boy wouldn't have fun doing that?

He immersed himself in the sheer delight of being on a spaceship, travelling across the galaxy. Montclair and Donna spent a lot of time showing him the ship's systems, and Monty even let him sit in the captain's chair.

Not even I had ever done that.

I knew Johnnie would be fine, eventually. He would return to his normal life and with time his young mind would heal and the nightmares fade.

∞

One day the ship's system interrupted us: "Excuse me," the ship announced. "Gurth has regained consciousness and is asking for Jack."

Montclair and I went to the medical bay and stood next to Gurth's bed. He looked around the room and then at us with weak eyes. "I take it that I am back on Montclair's ship?"

"Yes, and expected to make a full recovery," I said.

"You should have left me. I was prepared for an honourable death."

"That's not how we do things on Earth. If it weren't for you, Johnnie and I would have come to a very unpleasant ending. I wasn't going to leave you."

He continued to stare stoically up at the ceiling. I asked the question that had been bothering me since our escape. "How did you manage that, by the way?"

He looked at me. "Manage what?"

"Escape from the landing pod, then finding me in the ship. How did you do it?"

Gurth let out a long, slow twitter, that I'd come to know was how his people laughed. "Jack, I escaped the chains the Rajnack had me in. Did you really think your belt could hold me long in the pod?"

"Okay, sure. I didn't expect my knotted belt to hold you forever. But I did think it would keep you until we picked you up again."

"You were going to come back for me?"

"Of course. What do you take me for? But it was more convenient the way things worked out."

He turned his eyes back to the ceiling. I said: "But that doesn't explain how you found me, or why."

"A simple matter. I was a prisoner on that world for a long time, and I knew it well. I knew where the spaceport was, and that you would have gone there looking for your son. I went to the spaceport. The ship was right there. The same ship you had been chasing, and I'd seen it land on Orso's world. I knew you would have gone there looking for your son. When I saw the dead Rajnack lying on the ground at the bottom of the entrance ramp, I knew I'd found you."

"But how did you get up the cliff? There was a sheer rock face getting up to the spaceport."

"There are a few paths I know about from my time on that world."

"Why?" I asked.

"I don't understand."

"Why did you come for me?"

"To make amends for my actions on the ship, and to avenge myself on the Rajnack."

I placed a hand on his furry arm. "And indeed, you have made amends," I said.

Montclair grunted. "Easy for you to say, Jack. You weren't the one shot."

Gurth looked at Montclair. "My intention was just to wound you. I never meant to cause permanent harm or death."

Montclair frowned. "Well, am I supposed to be relieved at that? And then there's the small matter of the holes you put in my ship. You could have caused an explosive decompression, you know."

"I regret that. I don't own anything, but I will gladly make it up to you somehow. Maybe I could work it off."

Montclair got a thoughtful look in his eyes for a moment, then said: "We can talk about that later. But now that you are awake there is the small matter of what to do with you. We are on our way to Earth. Is there someplace you'd like to be taken?"

It turned out that Carimeth wasn't too far out of our way. Gurth asked to be taken there.

∞

We stood on the bare rock inside the enormous hangar Gurth's people had excavated deep inside Carimeth. It looked very much the way I remembered it. Rough rock walls damp with moisture. Whiffs of misty cloud against the rocky ceiling high overhead. A few other ships parked nearby, one of them unmistakably Radauti with its eccentric colouring.

Gurth was up and about again, albeit slowly and a bit stiffly with thick bandages around his waist. We gathered just outside the airlock of our ship to say our goodbyes.

"I can't thank you enough, good friends," Gurth was saying, looking like he might collapse from emotion. While not exactly his 'home' world, he was back amongst his own people for the first time since he had been a child.

"And I can't thank you enough Gurth," I said. "If it weren't for you, Johnnie and I would have died on that Rajnack prison world."

He nodded politely. The taxi arrived from town, a small hovercar not much bigger than a golf cart. "And now I must go," he said.

We finished saying our goodbyes. Johnnie gave him a big hug around the neck. They were both about the same height. Gurth needed some help getting up into the car. When he was situated he looked at us and said: "If you are ever in the neighborhood be sure to look me up."

We watched them drive off. "They still remind me of giant gophers," Donna said to me as she waved.

"Rabbits," I said.

She giggled and said: "The ears are too short."

"Let's see about some supplies and then be on our way, shall we?" Montclair said, a bit on the surly side.

"Sometimes you're just no fun Monty," Donna said.

A few weeks later we entered Earth's orbit. It felt good to be home again, even if I was facing almost certain imprisonment. We waited for nightfall over North America before dropping down from orbit to Beatrice's farm.

Chapter Eighteen

"He's a bit short to be one of your alien friends, isn't he?" Beatrice said as she gave Montclair a thorough looking over.

Montclair raised his eyebrows. "Madam, where I come from, I am not short."

"We'll, here you're short."

"Mother, stop it. You're being rude," Donna scolded. "Monty is sensitive about his height."

Montclair bristled. "I am not *sensitive*. I am merely trying to correct an error."

"Hmm, not sensitive huh," Donna giggled.

"Not all my friends are as tall as Gluplock and Xunathnick," I said to Beatrice, trying to suppress a laugh. Introducing Montclair wasn't difficult. She was used to having aliens over for coffee. Gluplock, Xunathnick and Worchisnick would often stay for a visit when they landed at the farm to pick up a load of coffee.

We sat in Beatrice's dining room, where she served us a hearty breakfast of eggs, bacon, hash-brown potatoes, and coffee. It was a welcome feast after weeks of tinned food. Johnnie was fast asleep in one of the guest rooms where he usually stayed when he spent the night.

The sun was just beginning to show itself over Beatrice's cornfields, flooding the kitchen with bright yellow light. The corn was high and almost ready for harvest. When we'd left Earth, it was the dead of winter. Donna and Beatrice had a few hours to hug and cry and weep on each other's shoulders, and another couple of hours to tell our story.

We finished breakfast and it was time to take Johnnie home to his mother, and hopefully not get arrested in the process. I asked Beatrice if I could use her phone. It was a 70's wall-mounted model with a rotary dial attached to a land line.

I dialled the number. Donna and Montclair looked at me with pensive eyes as I waited for the call to be answered. They looked almost as nervous as I felt.

"Yes?" came the answer. The voice was raspy and bitter.

"Gilda," I said. "It's Jack."

She was silent for a few seconds. I could almost see the ice crystals forming on the coiled telephone line between the handset I held and the telephone on the wall. After a moment she said: "Oh, how nice to hear from you after all these months."

"I've got good news..."

"The police are looking for you in connection with Johnnie's kidnapping, you know. Of course, you knew that. That's why you ran!"

"Listen, Gilda..."

"You are such a pathetic, no good, loser. Your son's been kidnapped, and you're hiding from the cops. They suspect that you know more about it then you told them."

"I had nothing to do with his kidnapping," I snapped.

"Don't raise your voice with me."

"Are you kidding? You practically accused me of being an accomplice. You know very well I'd never do anything like that."

"Oh, I know that. But do the police?"

"Just shut up and listen for a second. I found Johnnie!"

"Johnnie? You have him?"

"Yes, that's why I'm calling. He's with me now."

Her voice cracked with emotion. "Oh my God."

She started to sob openly over the phone. I just let her cry. After a minute or so she pulled herself together. "Is he all right?"

"Yes, he's fine. He wasn't harmed."

"Where?"

"Donna's farm."

"I want to see him right away."

"That's why I'm calling. I wanted to be sure you were home before coming over."

There was more crying on the other end of the line. "Where did you find him?"

"It's a bit hard to explain. But I've spent the last several months looking for him. That's why I haven't been around."

"Can you bring him to me now?"

"I'll be there soon."

I started to put the handset on the telephone cradle and disconnect when Donna jumped up and grabbed it from me. She put it against her head and said: "Gilda, this is Donna. Don't even think about calling the police on Jack."

Donna paused as she listened to the response. Then she frowned and said: "Is that so. Well, look at it this way. Jack, myself, and a few friends risked our lives and spent the last several months looking for him. Jack is a pretty big hero in Johnnie's eyes. What will that do to Johnnie if he sees his father being arrested when they get to your place, and what will he think of you when he finds out that you were the one who called the police. And I'll make sure he knows the truth if you do anything to hurt Jack."

Then she slammed the handset back down. She saw the way I was looking at her and shrugged. "I wouldn't put it past Gilda to have had the police waiting when you got there," she said.

I asked Beatrice to borrow her car. For obvious reasons we couldn't take the spaceship into town, and I didn't have any other ride. An hour later we pulled up in front of Gilda's bungalow.

∞

There weren't any police waiting. Gilda was at the front door when we pulled up and ran down the walk towards us. Johnnie jumped out of the car and they had a tearful reunion on the front walk. A few neighbors recognized Johnnie and started to gather around, talking and asking questions. We went inside for privacy and sat down in her living room.

I took a chair and Gilda and Johnnie sat on the couch across from me. Her place had been nicely repaired since the home invasion a few months ago.

Gilda hugged Johnnie and cried over him. Johnnie cried too, said he missed her, but he was finished with it all a lot sooner than Gilda.

"Mom," he said, trying to pull free. She kept a tight squeeze on him. He started squirming. "Mom, jeez."

She finally released him, dried her eyes, and leaned back. "How did you find him?" she asked.

Johnnie and I had rehearsed what to say on our way over. "I tracked his kidnappers to Bolivia, in South America. We found him there."

She covered her mouth with a hand and her eyes went wide. "What did they want with him?"

"That was never clear. I have no idea."

"Any chance these kidnappers will be back...again?" She asked, looking at Johnnie.

I shook my head. "We won't be hearing from them again. They've been...taken care of."

"Bolivia. Well, that explains why you seemed to disappear off the face of the Earth for months. How did you manage to track him?"

"I'm a detective, remember. It's what I do."

"This doesn't make any sense," she said, shaking her head and looking me in the eye. "Something's not adding up. Why come here for Johnnie?"

"I don't know Gilda."

"Well, the important thing is you're back now," she said, looking again at Johnnie. "Are you hungry? Want something to drink?"

"I'm okay. We had breakfast at Donna's."

Gilda shot me a dark look. "Oh? And how long were you there for?"

"Most of the night," came Johnnie's candid reply. Gilda's expression turned decidedly frosty. "You were at Donna's all night, were you?" She asked looking at me. "Why did you wait so long to call me?"

"We arrived at one in the morning," I said.

"You could have called me anytime day or night, you know that. I would have wanted to know. Instead, you chose to keep Johnnie at Donna's all night. He's my son, Jack. That doesn't seem right, does it?"

It's not all about you, I wanted to say. When we arrived back on Earth, all of us badly needed showers and fresh clothes. Beatrice washed and dried our clothes while we took turns bathing. Donna had clothes there, but Johnnie and I had to sit around in spare bathrobes that belonged to Beatrice and Donna until the laundry was done.

Afterwards, Beatrice prepared a feast for us. While in space we had nothing but the tinned food we'd brought from Earth and the space food from Montclair's ship, which was coloured paste in squeeze tubes and tasted about as good as it sounds. Eating Beatrice's home cooking, freshly bathed and wearing clean clothes, felt like heaven. And we wouldn't have had a chance to do any of that once I called Gilda.

But Johnnie was there, and I didn't want to get into a fight. So I kept it simple. "We were all exhausted from the trip and famished."

"I see," she said. But the corners of her mouth were turned down and she wasn't happy. But then, she always found something to be unhappy about, so I was used to it.

She patted Johnnie on the knee. "Maybe your dad would like some coffee? I know I would. Johnnie, would you mind going into the kitchen and making us a pot?"

He slid off the couch. "Sure Mom. Is there any juice? Can I have some?"

"Of course, sweetie."

Johnnie ran into the kitchen and Gilda leaned forward, placing her elbows on her knees. All business. Her eyes narrowed. "Who were those men that came in here and took Johnnie?"

I shrugged. Playing dumb was the only way to play through this. "I don't know Gilda. I have no idea who they were."

"Why were they dressed in those monster gorilla costumes?"

"Beats me. What did you tell the police?"

"I gave them a good description, of course. They weren't going to find Johnnie if I started lying to them, would they?"

"What did they think?"

"They just thought I was hysterical."

I didn't say anything. After a moment Gilda said: "I don't believe you would have anything to do with Johnnie's kidnapping, but this has something to do with you. It's connected to you, somehow. It's because of you they came for Johnnie. Revenge or something. Tell me I'm wrong."

I didn't say anything. She had me cold. After a minute she smirked. "I thought as much." Then she got up and walked over to a desk in the corner and returned with some papers.

She set them down in front of me, then went back to the couch. "Here's the deal. Sign those, and I don't turn you into the cops."

I flipped through them. "What is this?"

"Custody papers. I had my lawyer draw them up while you were away, just in case. I get one hundred percent custody, and you agree to stay away from Johnnie. In return, I keep you and Donna out of jail."

This was a curve ball I hadn't been expecting. I looked through the living room towards the kitchen where Johnnie had the fridge open. "You expect me to never see Johnnie again?"

"It's for his own protection."

"Not a chance."

She smiled. "The police already suspect you. If you don't sign them, I will change my story. You came in here, angry, and took him. I saw Donna in the car when you guys drove away. I'll make sure Donna goes to jail for a long time, just like you."

"You're crazy. It will never stick."

"I think it will. You're forgetting a few things. They already suspect you aren't telling them everything. You escaped custody with Donna's help. She drove the car you got away in. Later, they found her car abandoned at the spot where several witnesses saw you both get into a plane. She is clearly an accomplice."

"You already gave them a description of the kidnappers."

She grinned at me. "I was hysterical, remember. And I didn't want to implicate my son's own father. But now that I've had time to calm down and my head has cleared, details are coming back. Things I'd suppressed out of fear and shock. And several facts, as I've mentioned, will back me up."

"I'm not signing these."

"If you don't, I'll easily get full custody from a judge anyway, once you're in jail for kidnapping. Either way, I get full custody. And what will happen to Donna? It just depends on how badly you want to stay out of jail...and how much you want to protect her."

I didn't see that I had much choice. And I did have to go back with Montclair to his world, so I'd be away for a while anyway. I just didn't know how long. "You thought of everything, didn't you?"

"I've had a lot of time to think."

"If I sign this, will you clear me and Donna?"

She pulled out another large brown envelope and handed it to me. I looked them over. They were affidavits in Gilda's name, giving her version of the events that would clear Donna and myself of any complicity with the kidnapping.

I thought it over. In less than four years Johnnie would be old enough to live where he wants, regardless of what any court order said. Gilda probably hadn't thought about that, and I kept that thought to myself. The next few years would be tough, but we'd get through it.

"Sign those affidavits and keep Donna's name out of this, and I'll sign your papers."

She nodded, a triumphant smile on her face.

"I want to say goodbye to Johnnie first," I said and went into the kitchen, holding back the tears. Johnnie stood on a chair at the counter pouring water into the coffee maker from a glass measuring cup.

"Hey big guy. I'm going to leave you with your mom now."

He put the measuring cup down and hopped off the chair. "Are you going already?"

"Yes. I will be gone a while." I turned to look into the living room to make sure Gilda was not in hearing range. I said in a quiet voice. "I have to go back into space to help Montclair."

"How come?"

"Well, I made a promise that I have to keep. He helped me find you, so now I'm going to help him."

"How long will you be?"

"I don't know. Maybe a few weeks. I'll be back as soon as I can." I had no intention of staying away for as long as Gilda wanted. I'd figure out some way to see Johnnie when I got back.

I held him by the shoulders and looked into his eyes. "Remember what we talked about? You can't tell anyone what really happened. Especially Mom. No one will believe you and it will only get us into trouble."

He looked down at the floor. "I know. Boy, I've been in a spaceship and met real aliens and I can't even tell my friends about it."

"I know just how you feel," I said. "But you will always have Donna, Beatrice and me to talk to. And a few new alien friends." We hugged and said our goodbyes and then I left. I walked through the living room and stopped in front of Gilda. Johnnie was still in the kitchen.

She'd signed the affidavits. They sat on the coffee table in front of her. I picked them up and said: "I have to go away for a while, but when I get back I want to hear from the police that you've exonerated Donna and me, or I can make some trouble of my own."

She nodded, smiling smugly up at me. I bent down over the coffee table and signed the custody papers, then walked out.

CHAPTER NINETEEN

THINGS ONLY GOT WORSE on my way back to Beatrice's. I stopped at my place to pack some clothes and toiletries and some paperback novels. I didn't want to go into space again with only the clothes on my back.

I found a realtor's 'for sale' sign on the front lawn. My keys wouldn't work in the front door. A legal notice taped to the inside of the front window told me everything I needed to know. It had been repossessed by the bank for non-payment of mortgage.

I should have had plenty of money in my account to cover it. I made good money selling coffee to the Radauti and Donna and I were quite well off. Donna had paid off her mom's farm, and we were considering retirement. We'd talked about getting married, then going on a long honeymoon before returning home to begin life as a trendy young retired couple. We weren't sure what we'd do, but it wouldn't be detective work.

I stopped at my bank and found the police had put a freeze on all my accounts, in connection with the investigation into the kidnapping. That explained why the mortgage wasn't getting paid.

I didn't even bother going back to my office. It was just a rental, and I didn't have anything much of value. The landlord could have it all.

No money, and none of my credit cards would work. It was a good thing there was enough gas in Beatrice's car to get back to the farm.

It was almost noon by the time I made it back. Montclair had parked his spaceship in a clearing, behind the barns next to the cornfield, well hidden from the road and neighbors.

I found Donna and Beatrice in the kitchen, cooking and cleaning dishes. Donna looked great in summer sandals, light blue dress and white blouse; hair freshly shampooed. I stood in the doorway watching her for a few minutes before she saw me. "You clean up nice," I said.

She stopped drying the plate and smiled at me, then looked me over. "I thought you were going home to change."

"It's complicated," I said, and motioned to the back door with my head. "Can we go outside and talk?"

"Is everything all right with Johnnie? Did it go well with Gilda?" She asked as we stepped outside. The hot afternoon sun baked down on us. I could almost hear the grass drying in Beatrice's backyard. Montclair was nowhere in sight.

"Johnnie's fine. But there's something we need to talk about. I have to go away with Montclair for a while."

A look of worry clouded her cheerful expression. "Space?"

"Yes."

"When?"

"Today."

"Why?"

"I made a promise to Monty."

The look of worry began to transform into anger and frustration. "You mean, after all this, you're going right back into space! For how long?"

I reached out and gently held her shoulders. "I don't know, but it shouldn't be long. A few weeks maybe."

She pulled away and took a step back. "Are you crazy? After everything we just went through! We need some time together, I mean as a real couple, not as Mister and Missus Indiana Jones-in-space."

"I have to. I made a promise to Montclair to help him after he helped us get Johnnie back."

"This is nuts. What kind of promise?"

"Montclair needs my help to find some missing jewellery. He kept his end of the deal, so now I'm keeping mine. It shouldn't take long."

"Why didn't I know about this?"

"I guess it didn't come up until now."

Her face flushed red and she looked away, staring at nothing in particular while she thought. Tears welled up in her eyes. "I can't do this again."

"I'm not asking you to come with me. I don't expect to be away for more than a few weeks. Then I'll be back, and we'll talk about the rest of our life together."

She shook her head. "No, I don't mean that. I mean everything. I can't go through this anymore. When will this end? I can't sit around while you're somewhere in space, trillions of miles away, waiting for who-knows-how-long for you to return. I've been through this before, the first time you disappeared. I can't go through it again."

I took a step towards her, but she shook her head and put up a hand. I stopped and said: "This time it's different. You know where I am, at least in the general sense. And I'll be back before long."

"You don't know that. You don't really know how long you'll be or what will happen to you out there!"

"I'll be on Monty's world. It's pretty civilized, I'm told. I'll be fine."

"Easy for you to say."

We were silent for a few minutes while we stood looking at each other. Finally she said: "I'd take the ring off my finger and throw it back at you, except the Desert People already took it. But it's over Jack. I'm not going through this anymore."

She started walking back to the house. I grabbed an arm. "Donna," I said, pleading. "It's just a few more weeks. Then I'll be back, and no more trips."

She pulled her arm away. Tears ran down her cheeks when she turned to me. "I wish I could believe that, but it seems that with you something is always coming up. I can't spend the rest of my life waiting for you to return from space. I can't go through this anymore.

Goodbye." She turned and walked quickly back into the house before I could think of something to say.

∞

I found Monty sitting in the grass behind the barns, blowing smoke rings into the still summer air. The huge brass hull of the spaceship was partially visible from behind another barn not too far away.

He looked up at me as I approached. "Beatrice didn't want me smoking anywhere near her house."

I sat down on the grass next to him. "How narrow minded of her," I said. "Do you have one for me?"

Montclair handed me a cigar and a match. I lit it, turning it around slowly until it was lit properly. I blew some smoke, trying for a ring, but only managed a puffy cloud.

The way my morning had gone, it was certainly making it a lot easier for me to go back into space, much sooner than I normally would have wanted.

I felt crushed. Hollowed out inside. Donna had been the best thing that had ever happened to me, and I'd managed to screw it up. Although that wasn't entirely my fault, I reasoned. Gluplock and Xunathnick shared some of the blame for that.

But I had a promise to keep, so for now I'd go with Monty. I vowed to myself that I would return and find a way to win Donna back.

I'd be away for a few weeks, and maybe by then she will have cooled off enough to talk to me. I had to win her back. I couldn't imagine the rest of my life without her.

We smoked for a bit, blowing scented clouds up into the air.

"Well, Montclair," I said after a while. "We should probably be going."

Montclair made another smoke ring. "What about Donna? Did she want to come with us for another adventure?"

I shook my head. "Not this time."

"Hmm, that is too bad. We could use her talents. She's become an excellent pilot and I'd grown rather fond of her."

I attempted another smoke ring and failed.

"How are you set for cash, Monty?" I asked between puffs. "Something negotiable on Earth."

"I keep currency on hand for all the worlds I visit. It's necessary for provisions."

"Do you think we could stop someplace where I can buy some clothes, and maybe a razor, before we leave Earth?"

"Certainly. And I'm getting low on cigars. Without Donna, I'll be able to smoke in peace."

"Aren't there rules on spaceships about not smoking?"

"Not on mine!"

We finished our cigars. "Well, let's be off," Monty said. "I've got relatives back home who'll be worried. I've been gone too long. And the sooner we find that brooch, the better."

We got up and walked to the spaceship. Monty climbed up the ladder and into the airlock. I paused at the bottom of the ladder, and looked back at the farmhouse, hoping to catch one final glimpse of Donna. Then I climbed into the ship.

I closed the hatch behind me, wondering when I'd be back.

to be continued...

Jack and Donna's adventures in space continue in:

A Spaceship for Hire

Available on Amazon June 2024

Don't miss the next exciting sequel!

About the author

Mike lives in southern Ontario with his wife Pennie. They have six kids and a bunch of grandkids. He continues to write late at night and the wee hours of the morning.

You can contact him on his website or by email,
mike@mjwahl.com

www.mjwahl.com